Seb & Ailin: Case of the Murderous Mistletoe

Michele Notaro

Proofreading by Alternative Edits

Illustration and Cover by SEAJ ART

Contents

Chapter One

Seb

"How many kids are left on our list?" Ailin asked me as we walked out of a shoe store—one of our kids, Clover, had been talking about these specific boots she wanted for weeks. We figured that'd been a hint and added it to our Winter Solstice gift list.

I counted the names that weren't crossed off yet and sighed. "Ten."

Ailin, my partner and *viramore*—soulmate—groaned. "That many? Really? We've been here for hours already."

I shook my head. "We've been here for exactly seventy-three minutes, Mr. Dramatic."

"Yeah, but this is the fifth time we've been shopping for gifts."

"That's what happens when you have a billion kids, and those kids have kids."

He huffed. "A billion is pushing it, just a bit."

"Not by much."

He snorted and elbowed me.

Ailin didn't look a day older than his twenty-six years when we'd first met, thanks to those witch genes. And I didn't look a day older than my thirty-five—thank god. I had my enchanter genes to thank for that.

We might've looked fairly young, but the truth was that we had eighteen kids. When Ailin was sixteen, there'd been a horrible attack on his coven and all the adults were killed, leaving Ailin and fifteen younger kids the only ones alive.

Ailin had protected them from the enemy, and instead of sending his younger siblings and cousins into foster care, he'd stepped up as the head of the coven and taken care of them all. Aspen, Ailin's sister, was only a year younger than him, so she'd helped for a few years, but she'd already moved out of the house by the time I'd come into the picture. Ailin was the one who'd stuck around and raised them all as if they were his own children.

Because of that, we didn't count Aspen as one of our kids—but we did count Ailin's two younger siblings because they absolutely were our kids in every way that mattered.

When I'd come along and somehow slotted into place beside Ailin, the kids had accepted me as not only Ailin's partner but their other father as well. Ailin and I had eventually adopted three more kids because, apparently, fourteen hadn't been enough for our crazy family.

And then we brought our youngest son's best friend, Tan, into the mix. We never officially adopted him—not for a lack of trying—but he was still ours.

And now here we were with eighteen adult children who almost all had their own families, which meant we had grandchildren of all ages running around.

Being a witch had some amazing benefits, and not aging—or aging so slowly we'd hardly notice it for centuries—was definitely one of them.

Thank god being an enchanter came with the same ones, or I would've been a severely wrinkly old man standing beside my Ailin. And I had no doubt I would be beside him no matter what either of us looked like. We were soulmates, and even after decades together, I loved him more and more each day.

"Who's next on our list?" Ailin asked me.

I checked it. "Niya."

He groaned. "What crazy thing does she want this year?"

"She hasn't told us what she wants for years, A." I rolled my eyes. Most of our kids told us we didn't need to buy them anything, but we enjoyed giving them gifts, so we ignored them and did it anyway. "But I have rock climbing gear written down."

He rubbed his forehead and grunted. "That's right. I forgot that's what we'd settled on." We almost always got her some kind of gear for some adventure or another. Out of all of our kids, Niya was the most energetic and always needed to be doing something outlandish. "That girl is going to be the death of me one of these days."

"Same. But I think the sporting goods store is at the end of the mall, that way." I pointed to the right.

"Lead the way, baby."

We walked in that direction, side by side, both of us weighed down with several bags already. I heard a lot of commotion coming from the lower level of the mall, so I headed to the rail that overlooked it, just to take a peek. It didn't sound like anything was wrong, but if there was about to be some kind of supernatural attack, I wanted to be prepared.

A sigh of relief left me in a rush when my eyes landed on a big red chair with a man in a red suit sitting on top of it and a giant decorated Christmas tree behind it.

"What's going on down there?" Ailin asked me as he took a look as well.

I glanced around at the rest of the scene, taking in the hundreds of people—most of them were kids—and all the gifts sitting in a giant pile near Santa Claus. The kids were waiting in line for a chance to sit on Santa's lap and receive a gift while the parents took pictures and made their way over to the tables set up on the side.

The tables had a ton of Christmas decorations on them, and it looked like the parents were shopping for things. On the other side of the Christmas tree, there was a huge red carpet where kids were sitting and opening their gifts from Santa.

"This must be the mall's annual Christmas Gift Party Event. It's for low-income families. Not sure how they handle all that, but I do know that every family that shows up gets one gift per kid from Santa, a chance to shop at the decoration tables—but things are free or something; I think they get tickets—and they're allowed to take pictures with Santa. I didn't realize it was this weekend, but I guess that makes sense since Christmas is less than two weeks away."

Ailin eyed me. "How do you know about this?"

I sent him a grin. "People were talking about it the last time we stopped by Eastbrook." Eastbrook Youth Academy was the orphanage we adopted our three youngest children from. It also happened to be where I grew up, though it was about a million times better and a much happier place now, thank god.

"Huh." Ailin stared at the people below for a long moment before facing me. "That's a really nice program."

I sent him a soft smile. "Agreed." I leaned in and kissed his cheek. "Come on. We need to keep going or we'll never get done, and I don't want to have to spend another day shopping. We have way too many presents to wrap." We seriously needed all the time in the world to prepare for Winter Solstice, and we only had one week left to do it.

My phone rang right before we headed into the sporting goods store, so I grabbed it out of my pocket and smiled when I saw Tan's name on the screen. To Ailin, I said, "It's Tan." Then I answered with a, "Hey, bud."

"Hey, Seb," he said, and I could tell he was smiling. For once, someone wasn't calling us because something was wrong. I should mark the date on the calendar.

"How are you?"

Tan was our son, Remi's, best friend and didn't grow up in the best home, so he'd spent most of his teenage years in ours. Ailin and I had wanted to adopt him—not that he knew that—but his parents wouldn't agree to it, so we'd done everything we could to keep him at our house as much as possible. And when he grew up, we made sure to include him in everything we did as a family to ensure he knew he was one of our kiddos and very much a part of the Ellwood family.

"I forgot to write down the time for Winter Solstice, and I tried scrolling through the group chat to find it, but it's impossible. There's like five million messages since you sent the info out."

I snorted. Wasn't that the truth. The kids loved to text in the group chat, that was for sure. "We'll be there all day, obviously, so you're welcome anytime. But I think most people are coming between ten and eleven so we can do brunch." I followed Ailin into the store.

"Okay, got it. Thank you. I asked Remi, and he was no help whatsoever."

"That doesn't surprise me."

He chuckled, then paused for a beat. *"I'm... looking forward to having Garrick and Oakley come with me this year. I've never brought anyone before."*

My chest warmed. Tan had recently found his viramore, a dragon shifter named Garrick, who was at least fifteen hundred years old. And with Garrick came his twenty-something kid, Oakley.

It was unfortunate that Garrick lived on the other side of the world in Gauhala, but we were lucky that we had magical means of travel, so it wasn't difficult to get there. Ailin and I didn't know the dragon well yet, but he made Tan happy, so we were both happy.

If he ever did anything to hurt our kid, well, he would pay immensely for it.

"It'll be great. He came to a movie night last month, and it went well," I said as I continued to follow after A.

"True. But this feels different… I guess because it's a holiday."

I could understand that. "It means they're both a real part of the family."

He seemed to think about that for a few seconds. *"Yeah, I suppose you're right. We've made our own little family here, but including them with my family feels… important."*

"It is. And you know we love having them."

"I know." He cleared his throat. *"Anyway, I just wanted to say hi and ask about the time. Oakley's apparently dragging me to the store with them, so I should probably get myself ready."*

"Okay, bud. We'll see you next weekend, but don't hesitate to call if you want."

He let out a small laugh. *"I won't. Thanks, Seb. Talk soon."*

"Love you."

"Love you too."

We hung up, and I looked at Ailin, saying, "He's fine. Just checking in and asking about next weekend."

Ailin nodded. "I figured. You didn't feel upset, so I wasn't worried." Being viramores meant we were connected through our hearts, souls, magic, and minds. We could feel each other's emotions and even speak telepathically—sometimes that even happened accidentally.

I shot him a grin and gave him a shoulder-bump.

He waved at the display. "I have no fucking clue which one to get."

I stared at the gear with a frown. "Me either. Let's ask someone."

My viramore groaned but didn't hesitate to follow me through the store.

"**P**lease tell me we got everything," Ailin said as he set the last batch of bags on the living room floor. I'd asked him to grab all the gifts—not just the ones we bought today—so I could make sure we had everything.

"I think we did. I'm going to go through and double-check, just in case."

"Thank the Mother of All."

Snorting, I grabbed my checklist and a pen and started organizing all the gifts.

Three minutes in, my viramore plucked the notebook and pen out of my hands, ignoring my protests, and grabbed hold of my hips, tugging me close. His nose nudged mine before he rested our foreheads together and whispered, "Hi, baby."

"Hi." I closed my eyes and gave myself a moment to soak him in as I draped my arms over his shoulders. Maybe we had a lot to do, but he seemed like he needed the closeness, and honestly, I could use it too.

"We can finish this later, yeah?"

I grunted and gave him a small squeeze. "Yeah."

Ailin's lips brushed across mine, and I didn't hesitate to lean into the kiss and swipe his mouth with my tongue. He opened up, and our tongues brushed, making him moan into our kiss.

God, he tasted so damn good, felt so fucking good.

He gently pushed me back until my ass hit the couch's armrest. I spread my legs open, and Ailin stepped between them, pressing our bodies together. I ran my hands down his back and pulled him even closer, groaning when I felt his bulge rub against my half-hard cock.

A's fingers slipped under my shirt, and I shivered from the touch. Damn, I loved having his hands on me.

"I need you naked. Right now," he murmured into my mouth.

Just as he grabbed the hem of my shirt, his phone rang.

I whined, and Ailin said, "Ignore it."

We kissed, long, hot, and heavy, and my need for him grew. He said he needed me naked, but right now, I was the one who needed him naked and pressed against me.

Ailin lifted my shirt over my head, dropping it on the couch, and I went for his, but his phone rang again. *Dammit!*

Both of us sighed in defeat. If someone was calling twice in a row, there was usually a good reason for it. *Son of a bitch!*

Ailin pressed a chaste kiss to my lips, stepped away, took a long inhale, and pulled out his phone. "It's Alec."

"Fuck," I said under my breath as I grabbed my shirt, slipping it back on since I knew what was coming.

Alec was Ailin's brother-in-law and the head of the Brinnswick Central Agency. The BCA handled all supernatural criminal cases, and even though Ailin and I didn't work there full-time, we were called in as consultants pretty damn often.

Honestly, we should've just accepted the full-time positions they'd offered us years ago at this rate, but we'd wanted control over our work hours and over what cases we took—not that we ever said no to them. If they called us, they needed help, and as much as we complained about it, we also wanted to help keep people safe.

"What?" My viramore was so lovely when he answered phone calls—eye roll.

Since Ailin had the phone on speaker, I heard Alec say, *"I need your help."*

Of fucking course he did.

Sigh.

Chapter Two

Ailin

I sighed at the same time as Seb. "Of course you do. What's wrong?"

"*I've had over fifty calls from people saying their kids' toys are attacking them, and the calls keep coming in.*"

I blinked at that, then exchanged a look with Seb. "The toys are attacking kids?"

"*Yes.*"

"What kind of toys?" Seb asked, staring at me with wide eyes.

"*It's a variety so far, and apparently not only toys. Some holiday decorations have been attacking people too. The ones I've spoken to are all brand-new toys and decorations. But, guys, I don't have enough hands on deck. I've already called in everyone I can think of, and we're still having trouble keeping up. Can you please come help out?*"

Since this was for kids—and we always helped Alec out anyway—I didn't even have to ask my viramore. "Yes, of course. Text me an address."

"Thank you. I'll have you come to the same street I'm on. We set up a base here because there're several houses on this street with the same issue. Honestly, it feels like every damn house on this block has attacking objects."

"Okay, we're leaving now," Seb said, already nudging me toward the door. It was a shame I couldn't get him to stay shirtless while we were doing this. Seb glared at me. "No way in hell."

Oops. Guess he overheard my thoughts.

"Sera! Zamm! You coming?"

Our Bonded Ones—a familiar of sorts—hadn't wanted to come to the mall with us earlier because they'd been busy playing with some of the younger kids out by the lake on our coven land. But I doubted they'd want to be left at home for a second time today.

Sure enough, a tiny purple and black dragon about the size of a house cat came flying down the steps and crash-landed into the side of Seb's head.

"Oh my god, Zamm! What the hell?" Seb cried out, reaching up to grab the flapping dragon.

I stifled a laugh but didn't have time to tease him about his Bonded because mine, a black cat named Seraphina, came rushing down the steps and clawed her way up my body to ride on my shoulder. Damn, she had sharp claws.

Seb's Bonded might've had a rough landing, but at least she hadn't made him bleed, for fuck's sake.

We headed out, got in the car, and I plugged in the address Alec sent. Luckily, it wasn't far.

We arrived quickly but were cut off by a barricade. From the looks of what I could see, it was complete mayhem on the other side. There were people milling about everywhere with toys and decorations strewn about the yards and lying in the street. Some of the objects were on fire, some were lying on the ground destroyed and looking like something you'd find in a horror film, some were moving around, and some were underneath a witch's shield.

There were also several large shields around groups of people, keeping them safe. From the colors of the shields and the feel of the magic, I could tell some of my kids—Basil, Thayer, Jorah, and Clover—were already here and working the case. The four of them worked for the BCA, so that wasn't a surprise. There were some other witches and other beings with magic among the BCA agents as well.

Seb and I got out of the car and walked up to the barricade.

"Excuse me, sirs, but I'm going to have to ask you to turn around," a human police officer said. Alec had obviously called them in to help secure the scene. When he'd said all hands on deck, he'd clearly meant it.

I pulled out my ID while Seb did the same, then we both stepped forward to show the guy. "I'm Ailin Ellwood, and this is my viramore, Sebastian Ellwood."

The human's eyes went wide—we may've been a little famous since the Berserker War; our names were definitely written in the history books kids read in school these days—and he stammered. "Oh, I'm sorry... I... um... sorry, sirs, I, um, I didn't know. I—"

"It's okay," Seb said, cutting the guy off with a kind smile—he was always so polite and nice to strangers... at least when the strangers weren't a threat. "No big deal. But we're here to help out, so can we head in now?"

"Oh!" He quickly moved out of the way, waving us through. "Sorry. And, uh, thank you."

I had no idea what he was thanking us for, but I gave him a nod and weaved my way through the barricade with Seb right behind me and our Bondeds riding on our shoulders. No one even looked twice at the small dragon and black cat because everyone was used to witches carrying around their Bondeds this way.

That hadn't always been the case, but the Berserker War had many consequences, not the least being our grand reveal. Humans found out that magic was real and supernatural beings existed. Since many of those supernatural beings—including Seb and myself—had been trying to save all of humankind and the supe world, the humans had accepted us more readily than I'd expected. It took some getting used to back in the day, but since it'd been decades with us out in the open, no one batted an eye at our little Zammerra.

We headed toward a BCA tent on the side of the road. I figured Alec would be at the temporary command center, and if he wasn't, someone there could tell us where he was.

Luckily, we found my brother-in-law there, but he looked stressed as fuck. It took a lot to get him this worked up, so we were likely walking into a nightmare. Fun times.

"Hey, Al," I said as we walked in, giving Sera a few scratches.

He blew out a breath, looking relieved. "Hey. Thanks for coming... again."

I waved him off. "Alright, tell me where you need us."

"Let me call the kids over so they can tell you what they've found."

I might've been biased, but Alec generally wasn't when it came to work, so when he relied on my kids and said they were the best at their jobs, I believed him. Honestly, I knew they were because I'd worked with them too many times to count.

"Sounds like a plan."

He radioed them, and soon, Clover, Jorah, Thayer—along with his viramore, Toby—and Basil—with his viramore, Hiro—all came into the tent.

"Hey, guys," Seb said, then started petting Zamm, who was still wrapped around his neck.

I could tell he wanted to hug each of them as badly as I did, but we were all on the job, and there could be lives at stake, so we both refrained.

All of them lived on coven land, but they each had their own houses there with their viramores and kids. So even though they lived close by, we didn't see them every day. Although, all of our family members were in and out of the *big house*—AKA, my and Seb's home—all the time. I loved that they all came for visits, even if half the time it was only to come steal some food.

"Alright, tell me what you know," I said.

The kids all exchanged looks before Clover spoke up for the group. "So far, all we know is that a bunch of toys and decorations attacked people. We can all sense magic on them, but we don't know what kind of magic."

That's... unusual.

Before I could ask questions, Jorah added, "We can tell that the magic is sucking up the victims' fear and some of their life essence, but it doesn't feel like it's holding onto it."

My brow furrowed. "What does that mean?"

Basil shrugged. "It's like the toys are sucking in the energy and just letting it go—or maybe they're sending it somewhere else, but we can't tell where."

I blinked at that and exchanged a look with Seb before turning back to our kids. "You haven't been able to follow the magic?" All of them shook their heads, and I frowned. "That's... odd."

"Tell me about it." Bas sighed. "I think you should try. You might have better luck than we did."

My eyebrows rose. It was true that at one time, I was known as *Sage* and considered the most powerful witch in the world, but that was before Bas, Jor, and Thay sucked in the Power of Three magic during the Berserker War. They became *The Three*—also known as super badass and hella powerful witches with extra fae magic thrown in. Maybe my innate magic was stronger than theirs—but I doubted it since they were powerful in their own right—but with the added Three magic, there was no way in hell I had them beat, not even with the way my magic was able to combine with Seb's enchanter magic.

The title of Sage only stayed with me out of some strange sense of respect everyone had. I was pretty sure Jorah should've held that title, but no one wanted to listen to me about it, so there were still times people within the supernatural community called me it. I was used to it, so I answered to the title and shrugged it off.

"I'll take a look, but you know I'm not going to find anything different than you guys."

Thayer shrugged and shot me a smile. "Maybe not, but it's worth a try. You have a... better understanding of magic in general."

I stared at my kids, suddenly suspicious. I'd taught them all everything I knew, so there was no way all four of them had missed something, and they knew it. "Why are you all buttering me up? What do you want?"

All four of my kids laughed, and Toby and Hiro even cracked some smiles.

Jorah said, "We don't want anything."

"Uh-huh. I believe you." I rolled my eyes. Didn't want anything, my ass.

Seb said through our link, *They definitely want something.*

"Oh, I know. Little suspicious butts."

Seb snorted out loud, and Bas glared at us. "Stop making fun of us where we can't hear it."

I chuckled, and my viramore said mock-innocently, "We would never."

That made everyone laugh, and Bas gave Seb a playful push before we all filed out of the tent. Clover led the way down the street to a house that had a family of five standing on the front lawn, trapped under one of Clover's shields, protecting them. They seemed worried and scared but also grateful to Clover for her protection.

Clover walked over to them, reassuring them and doing a fine job of calming them down further. It wasn't hard to see how much she cared about people. She was such a good kid—not that she was actually a kid anymore, but she always would be to me.

Jor said, "There're some toys inside that we haven't disabled yet. We left them for you to examine."

I gave him a nod, then preceded the kids into the house with Seb right behind me. Our Bondeds hopped down to the ground, using their superior noses and ears to find the attacking toys or whatever they were. The front door opened up into a living room where there was a big Christmas tree in the corner, two couches, a TV, end tables, and a coffee table. But I didn't see any toys.

"They're in the dining room," Clover called out from behind me.

I grunted in acknowledgment and headed farther inside, walking under an archway that led to the dining room.

Seb yelled out, and I turned in surprise, expecting to see something attacking him, but a blink of movement above my head made me startle.

There was a flash of blue magic—Seb's magic—surrounding me. A shield. Seb had thrown a shield around me.

As soon as I had the thought, I saw a flash of green and red hit the top of the shield, right over my head. It made me flinch in surprise.

My eyes widened. On top of the shield was a piece of mistletoe tied with a red bow, but the mistletoe had sort of... come to life. And the thing was going crazy, wiggling around, flailing, banging against the shield again and again.

And it was... growling. How a mistletoe decoration was growling, I'd never know.

Going up on my toes to get a better look, I examined the crazed thing. "Ew." I wrinkled my nose. "It has teeth."

"That's disgusting." My viramore shivered dramatically. "How the hell did that thing grow teeth?"

"No idea, but it sure as hell wants to use them against me."

"No shit." Seb stepped closer and walked through his own magic to join me under the shield. "I thought I was going to have to catch it after it hit the shield, but part of it is still connected to the archway." He paused. "Well, if I wasn't going to have nightmares before, I sure as shit am now. What the hell is that thing?"

"No clue. Let me catch it with my magic so we can examine it."

"I'm not dropping my shield until you step away from that thing. If it touches you, I'm blasting it to bits."

That made me grin at him. I loved when his overprotective side showed.

When he saw the look on my face, he rolled his eyes. "Shut up."

I snorted and gave him a nudge until the two of us backed away, taking the shield with us.

That left the mistletoe dangling from one branch, swinging around, chomping at the air. I'd never admit it to Seb, but that thing was creepy as hell.

"Thanks for the save," I murmured.

"Like I'm gonna let some possessed murderous mistletoe attack you. Nope. Not on my watch."

I grinned again, but since I didn't want him to yell at me, I faced away from him so he couldn't see.

"I know you're smiling."

I couldn't help it. I laughed.

"Asshat."

Trying to shake off my amusement, I formed a shield that was open on one end, then wrapped it around the mistletoe, closing it against the ceiling. Seb dropped his shield without my asking, but I could tell he was on high alert, watching my back to make sure nothing else attacked.

With him—and the kids too—keeping an eye out, I let my earth magic out. It emanated from me in a green haze, and I gave it a tiny push toward the mistletoe, trying to get a sense of the magic within the decoration.

It only took me a few minutes before I paused. "Huh. That's weird."

Chapter Three

Seb

It was always nice to hear my viramore say something was weird when he was magically assessing something—*not*.

"What's weird?" Bas asked before I could.

"I... think this is some kind of curse, but I can't tell a hundred percent."

Bas cursed under his breath, and I said, "Well, shit."

"Yeah." Ailin sighed, and for a moment, he glanced down at Sera and Zamm, who were staring at the mistletoe, before he looked up at the kids. "You guys are right. It's pulling life essence and fear energy out, and then, seemingly releasing it out into the world. What the hell is this? Why would someone pull life essence if they're not even pulling it into themselves in the first place?"

"Maybe someone is nearby and collecting it?"

Ailin made a face, then turned to me. "I'm not sure if that's doable."

"What do you mean?"

"That's what's weird about it. Normally, in order to gain anything from fear energy or life essence, you have to be present when it's released and collect it straight from the source. I've never heard of anyone being able to collect it from a secondary location, or from midair, or anything. That's why it's never bottled up and sold. It can't be—nor should it. If someone tried, I'd shut that shit down immediately."

"Hm." I gave him a comforting pat on the back as I stared at the little monster, still going crazy and slamming against Ailin's shield. "That really is weird. What's the point of it, then?"

"Exactly. Why do this if you're not even gaining anything from it?"

"No idea."

"Which makes me think that someone *is* collecting it, but how?"

I shook my head because I had no idea either.

Ailin put his finger up against the shield, and we watched the mistletoe monster try to eat it as he spoke. "I thought that maybe this was some kind of prank, but a prank would stop at attacking toys and decor, right? Like... maybe someone thought it'd be funny to give people a scare. It sounds like something Bas would've done to his siblings on Solstice morning—"

"Hey! Why you gotta call me out like that? Any one of us could've done it."

Ailin glanced at Basil and raised his eyebrow. "Really?"

Bas glared, then rolled his eyes. "Whatever. Rude."

Before they could get into a full-blown argument, even if it wasn't heated and was kind of funny, I said, "What were you saying, A?"

Ailin sighed and refocused on the mistletoe monster. "I don't think this is a prank. A prank would stop at scaring someone, right? This... this is far beyond that."

I nodded in agreement. "Not to mention the scale of the attacks. I doubt a prank would involve over fifty families at once, right?"

"It's almost seventy now," Thayer said. "Alec's been sending the team updates."

"Jesus." I shook my head. "That's... a lot."

"Yeah, and they're still coming in."

I grimaced. This was awful, and there were already a lot of injured people. What if one of these things clung onto a child? What would happen? Could it kill them?

"Yes," Ailin answered my silent question. "One of these could absolutely kill a child. Hell, in the right circumstance, it could kill an adult."

"Fuck," I breathed out. This was not good.

Clover said, "Actually, there's already one teenager in critical condition. We have healing spells being sent over to the kid, so she should be alright, but yeah... this spell, or whatever it is, is really dangerous."

Ailin stared at our daughter. "Are you sure the healing spells will take care of it?"

Clover nodded. "Yeah, Dad. There's no internal bleeding or anything. She's just got a huge gash in a dangerous place, but we sent one of our healers to sew her up and give her the tonics. I'd tell you if they needed you to run over there and make a healing bed."

Ailin breathed out a long breath and gave her a nod before turning back to the mistletoe monster. Ailin was the best damn healer I'd ever seen, and he had the biggest heart of anyone I'd ever met. I wasn't surprised he wanted to make sure that teenager—a complete stranger—didn't need his help.

That was a part of why I loved the man so much.

Ailin nudged me with his shoulder without looking away from the mistletoe, so I had a feeling he'd overheard at least a part of what I was thinking.

After a few minutes, he sighed. "Alright, so I don't think I can follow the life essence. It's nearly impossible to see, and I have no way of marking it. Unless one of you has an idea?"

All of our kids shook their heads, and Thayer said, "We've got nothing, Dad."

Ailin nodded at him. "Alright, then all we can do for now is destroy all the toys and decorations that are cursed with this spell. I'm going to leave this guy"—he poked the shielded mistletoe—"shielded and with Alec so I can examine it better later. Right now, we need to get rid of anything that's attacking these poor people before more of them get hurt."

Jorah blew out a breath with a nod. "Sounds like a plan... but we're gonna be here all night. The count is up to seventy-eight already."

"Great," I mumbled. "After we kill everything, we've got to figure out where this shit came from and why this is happening."

"Long night indeed."

I scooped up Sera and Zamm, depositing the cat on my shoulder and the dragon on Ailin's since they wanted to switch it up this time. Then we all headed out, and Ailin pulled the murderous mistletoe monster along, inside a bubble of a shield, all the way to the tent.

"Alec, I need you to keep this one intact." Ailin floated the thing over to our brother-in-law.

"Why?" Alec grimaced at the thing as it tried to reach him through the shield. Those teeth were creepy as hell.

"So we can figure out what the hell's going on here. Right now, we're going to destroy all the attacking shit, and then we'll be back for that guy."

I said, "I'm going to bring back a couple more samples, just so you know. You might want to get some kind of container or something for it."

"My shield will hold, thank you very much." Ailin scoffed.

"Yes, but I think having it in something will make Alec feel better. Not to mention any of the victims that might come in here to talk to him."

Alec nodded. "He's right. I'll find a crate or a bin or something and throw it inside."

"Better get more than one. I want to have at least five more samples, just in case."

Ailin gave me a small nod. "Good plan, baby."

With a shrug, I led him out of the tent, hoping poor Alec would be okay with the murderous mistletoe so close by.

The first house we entered had multiple attacking objects. There were three toys—a stuffed bear, a train, and a handheld game console—and a giant wreath on the front door, all with teeth and claws and pulling fear and life essence out of its victims. It was gross.

Ailin and I caught the offending objects inside our shields, floated them out into the yard so we wouldn't destroy anything inside the home, and dropped them on the grass.

I pulled on my magic, and Ailin pulled on his, both of us forming nice-sized blasting orbs. Then we shot the shit out of the damn things until they were burnt crisps lying on the grass.

Zamm stomped on them, looking like she was doing a little jig as the flames died down under her feet. It was a good thing she was fireproof. It was honestly adorable, and I wanted to take a video of her doing it, but I didn't because of the severity of the situation.

When she was finished, I winced when I noticed how much grass we kind of... eviscerated with our blasts. *Whoops.*

In my head, Ailin said, *"Don't worry. I'll fix it."*

My viramore bent down, placed his hands on the ground, and I felt him pour his magic into the grass. It always amazed me how his magic worked. His magic gained its power from nature itself, but he could also push that power back into plants, trees, and flowers and help them grow strong and healthy.

Before I knew it, the blast marks were gone, and the entire lawn looked picture-perfect.

Since Alec had a clean-up crew coming in behind us to collect all the pieces of spelled objects as evidence, we left them where they were and walked to the next house over.

This one was much of the same, and I thanked our lucky stars that the humans in this home had time to get out before anyone got seriously injured. Here, there was a nutcracker, another teddy bear, a race car and track, a dollhouse, and a board game that had some serious strength when it came to snapping shut and trying to eat us. It could've easily chopped some fingers off—super gross and creepy.

We pulled the offending items out, destroyed them on the lawn, and Ailin fixed the grass before we moved to the next house and did the whole ordeal over again.

We did this for hours and hours until my feet felt like they were going to fall off and my brain was so tired I could barely string together two coherent words.

Our kids were still going at it, and every time we walked past them, I could tell they were as exhausted as we were.

"How many more?" I asked.

Ailin checked his phone since we'd been added to the update text chain. "Uh... three."

"That's it?"

"As of right now."

"Oh god, don't say that."

"You know more could be called in at any second."

I grimaced and gave him an angry look, even though it wasn't his fault. But he was right. We'd been down to two only an hour ago, and there was a sudden spike in calls, and fifteen more had been added on. This night couldn't get any more frustrating.

"Let's get this one done. Clover and Jorah have the one across the street, and Bas and Hiro have the one a block down."

"Fine. Lead the way. This better be our last fucking one."

He hummed in agreement, and we walked up the sidewalk to the next home on our list.

Right when we knocked, I felt my phone buzz.

Ailin went to reach for his own, and I grabbed his wrist to stop him, saying, "If we don't check it, we can pretend we don't know there's more."

He snorted and rolled his eyes. "Nice try, Seb. As if you'd ever not jump in to help someone who needs it."

I exhaled loudly.

"You know I'm right."

I shot him a glare. "No need to rub it in."

He snorted again, then tried the doorknob. It wasn't unlocked, which was strange. Every other house had been unlocked because the emergency operator had told everyone who called in with this issue to exit their home and leave the door unlocked for the BCA agents. But... maybe in their panic, the people who lived here forgot.

With no other idea what to do, Ailin knocked on the door again. We didn't expect anyone to answer since the family should've left the premises long before we arrived.

I called Alec, and after he picked up, I said, "We're at our last house, and the door's locked. What do you want us to do?"

"Uh, give me one minute. I'll see if I can find the family and get a key to you. What's the address?"

I rattled off the address to him.

"Got it. Give me a few. While you wait, why don't you go to the next one?"

I sighed. "There's really been more called in?"

"Only two."

"Well, at least that's better than last time. Let me know when you want us to enter this other house."

"Will do."

"Talk soon." I hung up and said to Ailin, "Let's go to the next house. We'll come back here afterward, and hopefully, someone will have a key or a way to open the door."

"You mean other than blasting it with your magic, which I know you're dying to do."

"I am not."

He gave me a look. "Sure you aren't, baby."

I flipped him off as we headed back down the sidewalk. Luckily, the next house was only three homes down. We entered and did our thing, taking out the garland, toy soldiers, and a stuffed elephant, fixed the grass, and headed back to the other house.

I called Alec again, and he answered with a, *"No one can find the family, so I'm gonna need you to enter the home immediately in case they didn't make it out. We have permission from Petunia Crane herself."*

Petunia was an old friend of ours who'd helped out during the Berserker War and was in charge of the council that ran the country. She'd been doing such an amazing job that people kept voting her back in. Although she kept claiming this was her last year—something she'd been saying for the last five years, so likely not. She loved her job, but she'd been doing it for a long time, so I wouldn't blame her if she needed a break from it.

Ailin liked to call her the Queen of Brinnswick, which she absolutely hated—that probably made him do it more.

Since I had my phone on speaker, Ailin could hear Alec as well, and he said, "On it. Call back in a few." He hung up my phone, and the two of us faced the door.

Since Ailin had more finesse when it came to opening doors with his magic—last time, I ended up simply blowing the handle off—I watched him pull power from the ground under his feet and release a green haze from his hand. The magic wrapped around the doorknob and floated into the keyhole, and only a few seconds passed before there was a soft *click,* and he was able to push the door open.

I threw a shield in front of us, just in case something came flying at us and attacked us, but when nothing happened, we stepped inside the house.

My eyes widened as I took in the living room, and I breathed out, "Oh my god."

Chapter Four

Ailin

S eb rushed forward, but I put my arm out to stop him. He opened his mouth to yell at me, but I said, "Hold on a sec. We need to figure out a way to safely remove it. Don't touch it. You might make it worse."

He was pissed—I could feel it—but he wasn't pissed at me. He was pissed at whoever had made these toys and Christmas decorations attack people. And I was right there with him.

On the floor of the living room, a man lay completely still, wrapped up in Christmas garland. It was so tight, I could tell it was constricting his breathing, and the guy was so pale he almost looked like a dead body. I was pretty sure the paleness was from all the life essence being sucked out of him.

How long had this man been in this position to look like that?

"How do we get it off, A?"

"I... I don't know."

Seb glanced around for a moment, then said, "Fuck it," and rushed out of the room before I could stop him.

I ran after him, but by the time I reached the dining room, he was already rushing out of the kitchen with a huge pair of scissors in his hand.

"Oh." Well, I suppose that might work, even though I'd been trying to find a magical way to help. I used my magic for pretty much everything, so sometimes I didn't think of the simple things, like using scissors. I was an idiot.

Seb knelt beside the guy and grabbed hold of the garland while Zamm and Sera stood on either side of him. Zamm was growling at the garland, and Sera was licking the guy's face, trying to wake him up.

The garland reacted to Seb's touch, twisting and turning its disgusting teeth on my viramore while the poor guy on the ground moaned in pain.

"Sorry, buddy, but I'm trying to get it off of you. Give me a sec." Seb slid the scissors under part of the garland while dodging the end that was flapping around and trying to smack him in the face. "Ow, you fucker."

He shook his hand out, and the moment I saw a drop of blood on his palm, I saw red.

I knelt opposite my viramore and grabbed hold of the garland with both hands, pulling as hard as I could. I ignored the sharp bites of pain and used every ounce of strength I had to yank that damn thing apart. I would *not* allow anyone or anything to hurt my viramore. I ripped at it, tearing pieces off with my bare hands while Seb continued cutting.

In only a couple of minutes, we had the damn thing in pieces on the floor, although it was still trying to attack us. With a grunt of annoyance, I used a bit of wind magic to sweep all the pieces into a pile, then gathered them into a ball and wrapped a shield around them. The pieces continued going nuts, but there was zero chance of them getting out, especially because I wasn't letting it anywhere near my viramore again. Fucking asshole Christmas garland.

"There. It's not getting out anytime soon." I turned to my viramore. "Let me see your hand."

Seb actually rolled his eyes at me, which made me frown. "For fuck's sake, A, I'm fine. But this guy on the floor, looking like death, isn't. Help him."

Oh. Right. "Right." I glanced down at the guy, then reached into my pocket and found a vial of healing tonic—the BCA had been supplying us with vials all night so we could help anyone we came across. "Sit him up some."

Seb lifted the guy's head, and I pushed on his chin to open his mouth, then I poured the healing tonic in. We made sure he swallowed it, and the guy coughed a little but settled when Seb put a couch pillow under his head.

"He'll be fine in a few hours. We need to check the rest of the house."

Seb stuffed the scissors in his back pocket with a shrug. "Might need them again or something."

"Right." I glanced at his hand. "You sure I can't look at your hand?"

"It's fine, Ailin. I'm not going to bleed to death from a tiny bite mark, for fuck's sake."

"You sure?"

"Oh my god, yes. Stop. We have more important things to do. The info packet said there was a man, a woman, and two kids in this house."

I grimaced, both at his lack of concern over his hand and the fact that there might be other people in this house. "If this guy is down here, hurt this badly, and alone, we can only assume the others are in similar predicaments."

Seb winced, stood, and hauled me to my feet. He quickly pressed his lips to mine and whispered, "I'm fine, A. You can put away your magic and calm down. I promise you I'm fine."

I blinked at that, then glanced around and realized I had a small windstorm of green magic floating around myself. I huffed and reined it in. When I became a little... overprotective of my viramore, my magic sometimes had a mind of its own.

Seb rolled his eyes and muttered as he walked away, "A little overprotective, my ass."

I ignored that because there really was nothing I could say to it since I knew he was right, and I followed him to the stairs. To Sera and Zamm, I said, "Protect him and let us know if anyone or anything else comes in here."

Sera sent back an affirmation. Since she didn't speak in the same way we did, she often communicated with me through pictures of things, feelings, and intent. It had taken some getting used to when I was a teenager, but it was second nature now, and I never had trouble understanding her.

It was eerily quiet up on the second floor, and I had a bad feeling about what we were going to find.

Please let them be alive. Please, please, please let them be alive.

Seb rushed into the first bedroom we came across with a shield in front of himself, but the second he walked inside, he dropped his shield and ran over to the body on the floor.

This one was a woman with long blonde hair with blood caked in it. *Shit.*

Since my viramore was checking on her, I scanned the room, looking for the culprit of the injuries. It only took me a few seconds to see a doll, probably eighteen inches tall, smashing itself against a... pillow beside the dresser over and over again. What the hell was it doing? Why was it attacking a pillow? Did the pillow... smell like a person or something? Did these things even have working noses?

And then I heard a small squeak of fear, and I rushed over to the doll.

As if it heard me coming, the thing's head turned around so it was facing backward—creepy as fuck—and looked at me... I mean, assuming the thing's eyes worked? Who knew? But it turned toward me, and all I could see on the creepiest face I'd ever seen was blood dripping from its mouth and splattered on its head.

I stopped in my tracks, a little freaked out, if I was being honest.

And then the thing came running at me. Its legs moved as if on the strings of a puppet, and it moved faster than expected. As it zoomed right for me, I let out a small shout, scooting backward as fast as I could.

Seb leapt over the woman lying on the floor to land beside me, and my viramore wrapped a shield around the doll in an expert move so quick, I hardly had time to blink. Then he turned to me and put his hand on my forehead as if checking for a fever.

"You okay, A?"

I blinked at him. "What?"

"You panicked there for a minute."

"It turned its head to look at me."

That only made him more concerned, and he stared at me for a few long seconds. "Are you... I can't believe I'm asking you this, but are you actually afraid of something?"

I wrinkled my nose. "No. Of course not."

That made him grin. "Holy shit! Ailin Ellwood, the great and powerful, is afraid of a little dolly."

"That thing isn't a fucking dolly, it's a monster."

He chuckled. "It's okay, A, I'll protect you from the little dolly."

The dolly in question growled, and I wrinkled my nose and took a step back.

And *that* made Seb crack up. "Holy shit, I can't wait to tell the kids."

"No. You're not telling them anything."

"You're scared of something—something that I'm not even scared of—and I love it."

That made me laugh a little. "When the hell did you become the ass-hole?"

"Always have been. You're just so much worse, you never noticed."

I gave him a playful smack to the chest. "Not true."

He smirked, waved me off, and gestured to the woman on the ground. "I gave her a healing tonic. She's covered in bite marks and has a big gash on the head, but I think that's from falling down and hitting it on the dresser."

I glanced at the dresser, noticing some blood on the edge, then startled. "Oh shit. I forgot."

"What?"

Scooting around the doll, I walked over to the dresser and knelt down beside the pillow the creepy doll had been attacking. Slowly, I moved the pillow out of the way and found a little girl, probably about six or seven, curled up behind the dresser.

"Hi, kiddo. We're here to help you. It's safe now."

When she saw me, she launched herself into my arms, crying and weeping into my shoulder.

"Shhh. It's okay. We've got you. You're safe now." She kept crying. "What's your name, sweetie?"

"Tabia."

"Hi, Tabia. My name's Ailin, and that's Seb over there." I rubbed her back soothingly. "We're here to help, but can you tell me what happened?"

"Mommy... she... hid... me, and it... it... it attacked... her."

"Shhh, shh, shh. It's okay. Your mommy's going to be just fine."

"She is?"

"Yes, sweetie. She's going to be alright. Seb there gave her a magical healing tonic, so she'll be back to normal in no time."

That made her cry a little more even as she said, "Thank you." After a few more sniffles, she said, "My brother... he's... he's in his room."

I caught Seb's gaze, and my viramore headed for the door. But I didn't want him going alone, and I didn't want to leave the little girl, especially since she was clinging to me like a spider monkey.

So I stood, hugged Tabia to me, and wrapped a shield around the both of us. I threw a shield over the top of the mom too, just in case. Then I skirted past the creepy doll, trying my best not to even look at the gross thing, and followed Seb down the hallway.

"Keep your head down, sweetie. I have a shield over top of us, so nothing can hurt you, okay? But I want to keep an eye on my viramore."

"Your... vitamin?"

Seb paused mid-step, turned, and pointed at me. "See? I'm not the only one."

I rolled my eyes but was amused. How anyone in the world could mistake the word *viramore* for *vitamin*, I'd never know. But apparently, Sebastian had all those years ago, and now, so had this little girl. If I didn't know any better, I would've thought he'd told Tabia to say it.

To her, I said, "No, my viramore. My soulmate."

"Soulmates are real?"

"They sure are, and even little humans like you can have one."

"Really?"

"Yep."

Seb entered another bedroom, and when I saw a teenage boy with the cord from his video game console wrapped around his neck, I sucked in a huge breath. But luckily for the kid, my viramore was on it. He pulled the scissors from his pocket and went to work cutting the kid loose.

To distract Tabia from what we were doing, I asked, "What's your brother's name?"

"Pietro."

"That's a nice name. What grade are you in?"

"First."

"Wow, that's awesome. Do you like school?"

She hesitated for a few seconds. "Most of the time."

That made me smile a little. At least she was honest.

It only took a few seconds for Seb to cut the teen free, and Pietro started coughing up a storm. But he was conscious, unlike his parents.

Tabia wanted to get down, so after Seb had the console in a shield and the young teen had drunk down a healing tonic, I set her down and let her run to her big brother. He grunted in pain when she slammed into him, but he didn't hesitate to hug her back and reassure her that they'd be okay. I could tell he was protective of her, so I knew she was in good hands with him.

I put the two of them in a shield and said, "We got the garland, the doll, and the video game. Was there anything else in the house that was attacking you?"

The kids shook their heads, and Pietro said, "That's it." His voice was hoarse, but the tonic should help with that shortly.

"Good."

Seb asked, "Do you happen to know where you got the toys and garland from?"

Pietro coughed a little, then answered. "From the mall. We went to some Christmas event earlier—or was that technically yesterday? I have no idea what time it is."

Seb gave the kid an apologetic shrug. "After midnight."

"Yesterday, then."

"Fuck," I breathed out. "That's the same answer we've gotten from everyone we've asked so far."

Seb looked at me. "At least we know where to start." In my head, Seb said, *"I can't believe that nice event we saw at the mall turned into this. What the fuck is wrong with people?"*

"I don't know, baby." I gave him a grimace, then put a call in to Alec. "Hey, Al, we need an ambulance or two. Both parents are unconscious, but they'll be okay once the healing tonics do their thing. We also have a teenage boy here that needs to be looked at. He's already had a tonic, but someone needs to make sure he's okay."

Pietro didn't look particularly happy about that, but he also didn't argue with me, so I took it as a win.

Alec said, "I'll have two ambulances sent straight to you."

"Thanks." I hung up, then squatted in front of the kids so I could ask them questions and keep them distracted while the EMTs got here and helped their parents.

It took a while, but the kids were loaded up in the ambulance with their mom, who'd woken up a tiny bit. They were taken to the hospital with their dad in an ambulance right behind them.

Once they were gone, we did a thorough search of the house, looking for any other magic or anything off, and luckily, we didn't find anything. So we pushed the shielded murderous holiday objects out onto the lawn.

As I stared at the creepy doll, I sighed and put my hand on Seb's wrist to stop him from blasting the damn things. "As much as I don't want to say this, I think we need to keep these guys."

Seb's eyebrows rose. "We do?"

"Yes. These three things were especially violent. Is that because they were actively attacking people for longer? Did they gain strength? Do they become increasingly violent as time goes on? Or is it because the person behind this upped their game when they realized we were shutting everything down? But we need to be sure so we can prepare for next time."

"Do you really think there'll be a next time?"

I blew out a long breath. "Unfortunately, yes. Because as far as I can tell, whoever's behind this didn't get what they wanted. We can only assume they wanted the life essence, but that's all... floating around in the air or something."

He grimaced. "True." He stared down at the toys and decor. "Are you sure you want to keep the doll?"

"No. But I think we have to."

I glanced at the thing again and gave a shiver. "Gross."

Seb snorted. "Alright, let's get these back to the others we collected throughout the day. Then we can head home, get some rest, and see what we can find."

I gave a nod of agreement. Then I called on Sera, who was walking around the house with Zamm. Both of them were double-checking our work and making sure we didn't miss anything. Using my bond with her, I asked her to bring Zamm here so we could all ride on her back on the way to our car. That would be so much more fun than walking back for ten miles... or however far away we were.

Chapter Five

Seb

Zamm shifted to one of her larger dragon sizes, and I was a little surprised that Sera didn't shift into her manticore form because the two of them usually liked to fly together. Instead, she climbed onto Ailin's shoulder, gave his cheek a nuzzle, and meowed at me in a way that I knew meant, "Get your butt moving."

So... I got my butt moving and climbed onto Zamm's back. We had a saddle for her at home, but it wasn't necessary, especially for a short ride. There was a natural dip where her neck met her shoulders that was perfect for sitting on. And she didn't mind when I held onto her spikes while she flew. I'd ridden on her back enough times to be somewhat of an expert. So had Ailin, for that matter.

We'd borrowed a sheet from the house, and keeping the cursed objects inside their individual shields, we wrapped them up in the sheet to make them easier to carry. Zamm agreed to grab the sheet for us, and I was grateful since that meant the scary doll would be farther away from Ailin. The last thing we needed was him freaking out midair.

Ailin climbed on behind me and nestled up to my ass in a way I knew he was doing on purpose to get a rise out of me since we were still in public. I wiggled around a little, making him groan, and I smiled to myself.

"Proud of yourself?" he asked.

"Yep."

He snorted in my ear, and I felt Sera settle on his lap so she was held between us and couldn't fall off.

Once Ailin wrapped his arms around me, I said, "We're ready, Zamm."

My Bonded stood and grabbed hold of the sheet of cursed objects in one of her taloned hands. Then she squatted down before launching up into the air. Before she could start to fall back down, she opened her wings to catch the draft, gave them a mighty flap, and we were up, soaring in the air.

Ailin rested his cheek against my back, leaning over the top of Sera so he could reach me. I honestly couldn't wait to get home, put on comfy clothes, climb into bed, and wrap him in my arms.

In my head, Ailin said, *"Me too, baby. I'm so done with this day."*

"We're just grabbing the other cursed objects and leaving, right?"

"Right."

"Do you really think it's a good idea to bring those things onto coven land?"

He was quiet for a few seconds, clearly thinking things over. *"We have all those things in the basement, and half of them are more dangerous than these things. We can keep them shielded in the basement while we sleep."*

He had me there. We had a number of magical items that we'd deemed too dangerous for use in our basement. When a dangerous magical item appeared anywhere in Brinnswick, we were usually called in to take care of it. Unfortunately, many of those things were too powerful to destroy, or they held too much history for us to destroy them in good faith.

Ailin had been collecting things like that since long before I met him, and I supported him in this venture because he was making the world a safer place.

That didn't mean I liked having those things in our home, though.

But I also knew they were in the safest place they could be, *and* they were shielded and safeguarded to high heaven. There really wasn't a better place to take the damn toys and Christmas decorations.

"Yeah, okay. That's fine. I just worry."

He kissed the back of my neck. *"I know you do, but I'll keep you safe."*

I snorted. *"I'm pretty sure it'll be me keeping you safe if those things attack us. You were terrified of that doll."*

"It turned its head so it was backwards and looked at me with blood coming out of its mouth and all over its face!"

I couldn't help but laugh. I'd seen this man go up against so many other things that were absolutely terrifying without even blinking, like giants, literal giants, and huge-ass sea monsters, and evil rougarous, and zombie-like huge-ass ogres. And here this little dolly was the thing that scared him.

"Shut up!"

I continued laughing. *"After all the shit you've given me about being scared of snakes and spiders, I'm planning on milking this for a very, very long time."*

He grumbled and rested his head on my back, and I just kept laughing. I couldn't help it. He wasn't actually angry or upset. In fact, I was pretty sure he was a little embarrassed but mostly amused by my amusement.

Not that he would admit that out loud.

It didn't take long for us to fly over the first street we'd started on where Alec's tent was still set up, and I couldn't help but frown down at it. Nearly every house had a pile of toys and decorations on their lawn, lying in ruins. It was really damn depressing, honestly.

"I feel bad for all the kids that lost their new toys," Ailin said, clearly on the same page as me.

"Me too. And they were gifts from Santa... that makes them special."

He sighed, and after a few seconds, he gave me a squeeze. "We could... maybe buy them new toys—that we make sure aren't cursed or whatever—and give them out to the kids."

That made me smile, and I wasn't the least bit surprised by this. My viramore was always trying to help people, and when it came to kids, he went above and beyond. Ailin and I weren't the richest people in our country or anything, but we definitely weren't hurting for money either. "I'd like that."

"Okay. New plan. Go home, sleep, wake up, eat some food, go to the mall to question them, buy a ton of toys, and hand them out to the kids. We can have Del and some of the other kids start examining the cursed objects while we're doing all of that because we need more people on this anyway. We'll leave Del in charge." Our son, Delaro, was very into experiments and would jump at the chance to help out, especially since he'd be exploring something we hadn't seen before.

"Sounds great."

After we touched down, collected the rest of the spelled Christmas objects, and got in the car—with Ailin driving—I pulled out my phone to send a text in the family chat.

Me: Just wanted to tell you guys that Dad is scared of a little dolly.

I attached a picture of said dolly, then sent it off. It didn't take long for the kids to start texting back.

Opal: To be honest, I think I'd be afraid of that thing too. Ew.

Tio: Are you sure Dad's scared of it? Can't he just like blast it or something?

Me: Definitely terrified. He even screamed. It was amazing.

Thayer: Please tell me you have that on video.

Me: Unfortunately no, but we're bringing the doll home, so you'll get to see it for yourselves.

Bas: Priceless.

Clover: That thing is gross. Can't wait to see it.

Del: Is that blood on its face?

Jorah: Probably. Toys have been attacking people... with teeth.

Del: Ew. I want to see it.

I snorted at that. Of course he wanted to see it.

Bas: Can we let that thing out of its shield and see what Dad does?

Niya: Yessss. I vote for yes.

Thayer: Me too.

Jorah: Me three.

Opal: We're recording it! And it has to be a sudden drop of the shield. We gotta surprise him.

Niya: Try to make him scream.

Willow: That sounds hilarious. I'm in.

I chuckled as the kids continued making plans on how to scare Ailin, even though it was in the family chat... which Ailin was a part of. I'd feel bad except Ailin had been letting the kids scare the shit out of me with snakes and spiders for years. Payback was a bitch.

"Why are you laughing so evilly over there? I have to assume it has something to do with how much my phone is buzzing?"

My laugh grew. "Oh, A, you're going to be hating life later."

He glanced at me, then let out a long sigh. "You told them about the fucking doll, didn't you?"

"Sure did."

"So glad you're so proud of yourself over there."

I snorted and reached over to pat his thigh. "Thanks, babe."

He snorted and shook his head, but I could tell he was reluctantly amused.

Chapter Six

Seb

The next day, Ailin and I wanted to go to the mall where all the toys and decorations came from, but Basil, Jorah, and Thayer convinced us to let them handle that while we bought toys for the kids—and made sure they weren't cursed or unsafe.

Ailin had grumbled a bit, but he was trusting the kiddos to do their job—which was kind of a big deal. My viramore was stubborn and usually wanted to do absolutely everything himself, so this was a nice change. Plus, the kids were good at their jobs and didn't actually need us to do it for them.

So far, the kids had gotten the name of the store that had donated many of the items for the mall's Christmas Gift Party Event, and they were heading there now. The mall received other donations, but this place supplied the most, so it was our best bet on where the cursed objects had come from.

As much as Ailin had let the kiddos take care of it, he'd been constantly demanding updates from all of them. It was kind of ridiculous, but the kids were handling it like old pros—handling *him* like old pros, I should say.

I reached across the center console of our minivan and grabbed his hand, stilling it from where he was currently texting the kids. Again.

"They have it under control, A."

He let out a long, drawn-out sigh. "I know they do. I just…"

I gave his hand a squeeze. "I know. But we're doing something good and worthwhile, right? There isn't much else we can do right now until we have a lead to follow, anyway. The kids said they'll call us if they find anything good."

He sighed again but pushed his phone into his pocket. "Fine. I'll… let them be… for now."

I gave an amused shake of the head, but at least I'd gotten him to chill out for a few minutes. I knew it wasn't going to last, but I'd take the small win.

Ailin's give-kids-presents-plan worked out pretty well. We basically bought out an entire toy store this morning—a different place than where the kids were going. And now we were on our way to the safehouse Alec had set up for all the victims of last night's attack. It was just a few old warehouses owned by the government that they added a ton of beds to for the night. It wasn't glamorous, but it was all the BCA could provide with such short notice.

From what Alec had said last night, they were planning on having the families stay there for one more night before letting them back into their homes. If they had to stay longer than that, the BCA would've found actual homes or at least motel rooms for everyone, but since it was so quick, this would do.

I parked our minivan, which was absolutely packed with toys, and the two of us and our Bondeds got out.

Opal, one of our kids, parked her minivan beside our own. On the other side of her van, our other daughter, Niya, parked her SUV. And our son, Tiordan, parked his SUV beside our van.

All of their cars were also absolutely packed with toys.

It was ridiculous.

But also... awesome.

I was so happy we were doing this, although it sucked that we couldn't wrap the toys up first. But we didn't have time since we needed to get back to investigating and stopping whoever had done this in the first place.

Opal sent me a smile. "I guess we should start carrying everything inside."

I sucked in a breath and nodded. "Yep. Let's do this."

Everyone grabbed as many toys as they could carry, and we headed inside. We piled them off to the side, then went out for more while Zamm and Sera ran off to find some kids to play with. They *loved* running around with kids, which was the whole reason they'd even wanted to come with us today. I didn't mind—it was fun for them and the kids both.

Honestly, who wouldn't want to play with a small dragon and a cute kitty?

Just when we were finishing up, Alec parked his car in the lot, hopped out, and came over to me. "I would've gotten here sooner if I knew you needed help."

I waved him off. "It's fine. We're nearly done. What're you doing here?"

"I'm checking in on my people who've been conducting interviews with all of the victims. It's... a lot. I've been going back and forth between here and over to our temp HQ at the site since last night. And to top it off, I got a call that a few of the people here were giving some of the officers a lot of grief. I came to smooth things over and explain why they can't go back to their homes yet. We're still collecting evidence and making sure it's safe. We need a little more time."

"Honestly, I think two days is pretty damn impressive. You guys move fast."

"Only because we have some powerful witches on our side speeding up the process."

I smiled at that. "That'll do it."

He smacked my shoulder, grabbed a pile of toys out of Tiordan's SUV, and walked inside with us.

Sera and Zamm went zooming past us with a trail of giggling children running behind them, making me chuckle.

Ailin gave Alec a nod before coming over to me as I set the toys down. "How do you want to do this?"

"Well... I guess we should tell the parents to bring their kids to this warehouse since there are some in the other two next door, then make a line. Why don't you stand there, and you can talk to the kids and hand out toys. One of us will grab whichever toy the kid needs and pass it to you, I guess?"

Ailin nodded. "Let's have another person talking to the kids and handing out the toys to make it go a little faster."

"Sounds good." I turned to the kids. "Who wants to hand out toys?"

Niya and Tio both turned to Opal. She gave a shrug, then stepped up beside Ailin. "I'll do it."

Ailin gave her shoulder a pat, shooting her a small smile that she returned.

With a smile of my own, I nodded at her. "Perfect. Should we let the kids decide what they want?"

Ailin shrugged. "I have no idea, but I guess we can try it that way and switch it up if it's not working."

"Sounds like a plan. I'm gonna grab a couple of chairs for us, just in case we need them." I gave Ailin's hand a squeeze before walking past him as he went to ask the parents to spread the word.

There were already a bunch of kids sitting close by, eyeing the toys, so I figured it wouldn't take long before there was a long line.

A woman came up to me, asking, "Are you sure these toys aren't going to do the same thing as the other ones?"

I smiled at her. "We're one hundred percent sure. We had five different people check them over, using several different magics. No one detected a thing, and we inspected the other toys enough to make sure we knew exactly what we were looking for. I promise these are safe."

She made a face, and I could tell she still wasn't sure.

Since I had no better idea, I added, "They're Ailin and Sebastian Ellwood approved."

I wasn't sure if the people here knew we were the ones doing this yet, and well... our names held clout after everything we'd been through and everything we'd done to keep Brinnswick safe. Hopefully, knowing we were the ones who checked over the toys would help put her at ease.

She blinked at me for a moment before her eyes widened. Her gaze swept over me, then over Ailin before swinging back to me. "You're..."

I gave her a small smile. "I'm Sebastian. Ailin's handing out toys over there." I pointed at him. "It's nice to meet you."

"Holy shit," she breathed out quietly in a way I knew I wasn't meant to hear, so I pretended not to. After a brief hesitation, she blew out a breath and gave a single nod. "Alright. Thank you. We all really appreciate everything you guys are doing for us."

"Of course. It's our pleasure." And honestly, it really was. Giving out toys to kids was a lot of fun and made my heart happy.

I set a chair behind Ailin so he wouldn't have to bend over constantly to hear what each kid wanted, and he sent me a grateful smile as he listened to a little girl's request.

When she finished, he turned to Niya, saying, "A doll with red hair, if we have one."

"Coming right up," Niya said, going back to the giant pile of toys.

I nudged Ailin as I walked past him. *"You sure you can handle giving her that doll? You aren't too scared? I can come sit in for any and all doll requests if you want."*

"Shut it, asshat."

I laughed out loud.

In all the years I'd known him, he'd never been afraid of dolls. He'd always been fine playing with dolls with all of our kids and grandkids. But I had to wonder if he'd want to stay away from them after last night.

Shaking my head, I concentrated on helping organize the toys to make it easier to find what we needed so we weren't here all day long.

About an hour in, I figured this would end up taking way longer than I expected. But at least the kids were really happy, and some of our kids were still studying the spelled objects at home, so it wasn't like this was a waste of time or anything like that.

Alec came over to say his goodbyes, but before heading out the door, he nodded toward Ailin and said, "He's really in his element, isn't he?"

I turned to see what he was looking at.

Ailin was kneeling in front of a young girl, talking animatedly and making the girl giggle. Niya handed him a toy, and when he passed it over, the little girl gave him a hug around the neck. He laughed and patted her on the back, then booped her nose when she released him.

As soon as she moved away, a young boy took her place, and Ailin looked just as happy talking to him as he did with her.

"He really is," I replied. "He loves kids." I glanced at Alec. "You know, if he ends up wanting another kid after this, I'm blaming it on you."

He barked out a loud, deep laugh. "On me? I'm not the one that decided to buy all these kids toys."

"No, but you're the reason we got involved in the first place."

He huffed. "Maybe, but it's still not my fault if he wants one."

"Yes, it is, and if he does, you're taking *alllll* the babysitting duties."

He snorted. "Does that mean you don't mind if he wants more? You're willing to adopt more kids?"

I grimaced a little. "I... no. I don't particularly want more—I like having my viramore all to myself now and not having to make babysitting plans—but I... think he could probably convince me. I mean, hell, he convinced me to let all those thunderdogs in my house before. He could probably convince me to do anything—don't tell him I said that. God, don't ever repeat that. *Ever.*"

He held up his hands, looking amused. "I promise I won't. But, man, you're so coming out of this with more kids. Just look at him."

I pursed my lips. "Maybe I can get him a puppy or something instead."

Alec snorted and patted my back. "Good luck with that. I'll see you later. Call me if you guys find anything."

"Will do. See ya."

I sighed and simply watched my viramore play Santa Claus for a little while longer, keeping my fingers and toes crossed that he didn't come home and try to convince me we should adopt more kids.

Eighteen was enough, for fuck's sake.

Chapter Seven

Ailin

I wonder if I could convince Seb to adopt more kids with me.

It would probably be a hard sell, but I could maybe do it.

I glanced over at Seb standing there with his arms crossed and a frown on his face. Mother of All, he was handsome.

And he looked fucking cute when he was all angry, although what he was angry about, I had no idea.

Annndddd... he likely overheard my thoughts about adopting kids, and that was probably what put that grump on his face. *Sigh*. Maybe I wouldn't be able to convince him then.

As soon as I handed the last kid his toy and he ran off, I stood, stretched, and walked right over to my viramore. I wrapped my hands around his waist, went up on my toes, and pecked his grumpy mouth. He sighed like he was annoyed, but he wrapped his arms around me, gave me a chaste kiss back, and pulled me into a hug.

"You made those kids so happy," he murmured.

"*We* did. And everyone that helped us. It wasn't just me."

"No, but you're the one who played Santa Claus—well, you and Opal—so you're the ones who they'll remember."

"Fair enough." I kissed his cheek and stepped back. "I guess we gotta go home and see what Del's come up with."

"Sounds good. Let me just leave the extra toys with someone who can give them out in case we missed anyone or if people come in late."

"What about the kids that are in the hospital? I don't know if we have time to go all the way there today, but..." I shrugged.

He sent me a smile. "I already talked to Opal about it. She's going to grab Laneo, and the two of them are going to head over to the hospital today."

Laneo was a sky fae from Faela—the land of the fae, which was in another realm—and also happened to be Opal's viramore. He was a sweet guy who'd been a part of the family for a long time now.

I didn't know why I was even surprised that Seb had already thought of that. "Great."

"I texted Del about an hour ago to see if he had any news, and I got the feeling he's having trouble with the cursed things."

I eyed him. "Really?" Delaro was the best at work like that, so if he couldn't find anything, we were pretty much screwed.

"Don't say that to him. You know how hard he is on himself. He'll blame everything on himself."

I winced. Clearly Seb had overheard my thoughts. "I would never say anything like that to him."

"I know." He gave me a nod, then shoulder-bumped me as we stacked the extra gifts against the wall. "We really need to find some time to wrap our Solstice presents. We have absolutely nothing wrapped yet."

"I'm aware." I blew out an annoyed breath. "After we figure out who's behind this, we'll spend a day wrapping."

"As if we ever have a whole day we can dedicate to anything."

And that was... fair. With as big a family as ours, we were kept very, very busy. "True enough, baby. Maybe we can concentrate on wrapping all the grandkids' stuff first, then move on to our kids. If we run out of time, we can always throw stuff in bags."

"I hate using gift bags for Solstice."

I had no idea what his beef was with gift bags, but it was a thing twenty years ago and it was a thing now. "Needs must."

He sighed and waved me off. "Better than nothing, I guess."

"You're so picky."

"Look who's talking."

I snorted. "Me? Don't be ridiculous."

"You sure do think high and mighty of yourself, don't ya?"

"Yeah, that's me, Ailin the High and Mighty."

He chuckled, and from behind us, Tio said, "You guys are so weird."

I sighed. "Of course *that* would be what you hear."

Seb laughed a little harder, then pulled our son into a side hug, saying, "Don't look at me. That was all your dad."

I elbowed him with a laugh, making Seb snort and Tio shake his head in exasperation at us.

Soon enough, we were heading back out to our cars, and I gave Opal, Niya, and Tio each a hug, thanking them for their help today.

Niya waved me off when I thanked her. "You don't need to thank us, Dad. You know we like helping out with stuff like this."

I smiled at her. She was right. All of the kids liked helping us do things like this, and Niya volunteered at all of the adoption events held by Eastbrook Youth Academy—the place we adopted her from. Most of my kids helped out at least a few times a year at their events, but Niya and her viramores were steadfast in their volunteering, and I was pretty sure she'd only missed a handful of events since she turned eighteen.

Which was way longer ago than I wanted to admit.

I pulled her into a second hug, and she grumbled a bit but didn't pull away. Then I kissed her temple and released her. "Alright, pumpkin, let's head home."

She shot me a smile, then hopped into her vehicle and headed toward coven land. Like most of my kids, she didn't live in the same house as me anymore, but she did live on coven land—the safest place on earth—with her *three* viramores. Honestly, she needed that many people to keep up with all her hyperness. The four of them made a good team.

Seb climbed into the driver's seat, I got in the passenger's, and we followed our kids out of the parking lot. When I placed my hand on Seb's thigh, he shot me a smile and set his hand on top of mine, giving it a squeeze.

"You doing alright?" he asked me after a little while.

"I'm good."

"You're awfully quiet."

"Just thinking about all those kids and about the cursed toys that attacked them and stuff." I shrugged.

"Wanna talk about it?"

I sighed, then ground my teeth for a few seconds as I thought about this entire shitty situation. "I hate that all of those people were in danger. We need to find the bastard that did this and stop them, and we're just... failing at that. It's pissing me off. We did good today, but if we can't stop this asshole, then everyone's still screwed. For all we know, he's already planning another attack."

He lifted my hand and placed a kiss on the back of it. "We'll figure it out, sweetheart, and at least they're all safe now."

I nodded in agreement. I knew we would... eventually, but I was worried someone would be killed if more toys attacked people. We were very lucky that no one had died yet, but I had a feeling we wouldn't be that lucky in the future.

Once we made it home and parked the car, we got out and headed toward Delaro's house. Originally, we'd wanted to keep the spelled objects in our basement, but Del had taken them to his workshop, which was bigger than his house at this point. It was still on coven land, right across the yard from his house and just a short walk from ours.

When we walked into his workshop, I wasn't surprised to find Nikolai and Grayson inside, assisting our kiddo. Sometimes, I still found it hard to believe that Delaro had two viramores *and* that one of them was Nikolai.

I loved the guy now. He was family, but if someone would've told me that back when I first met him, I never would've believed them. He'd always been so... devious, or at least he'd given that impression. Now I knew he was a kind, caring, and loving man.

And Gray was a great guy too. He was a gentle giant and a sweet guy who obviously loved Del and Nik and their kids very much. The three of them worked well together.

But that didn't mean I had to tell them that.

When Seb and I reached the other side of the building where they were, I said, "Nik. Gray." I gave them each a nod, then turned to Delaro. "Hey, kiddo."

Del met my gaze, then rolled his eyes, amused by my less-than-thrilled greeting to his viramores. "Hey, Dad. Pops."

I sometimes missed the days when the kids called Seb *Papa*. I understood why they'd stopped—they were too old for *Papa*—but Seb and I both missed it a little since it was the first parent title the kids had assigned him. Seb thought *Pops* was cute, though, so that was good.

Seb, being the kind and sweet man he was, walked over and gave each of the men a hug. I normally did too, but I suppose I was in a mood because, from the look on Del's face and the lack of messages throughout the day, I could only assume we still didn't have any answers.

Which meant everyone, literally everyone in Brinnswick, was in danger of being attacked again.

Sonofabitch!

"Any news, Del?" I asked after all the hugs were done.

Del grimaced. "Well, it isn't ghosts. But you already knew that."

Seb sighed. "Does this mean you don't have new information?"

"Pretty much. I can't sense anything different whether I'm in this plane or the ghostly one."

Because of Del's Bonded, Zig, the two of them were able to hop between our plane and the ghostly one. Zig was a bakeneko, which was a kind of cat spirit, although he had a physical form... when he wanted to. Del had been utilizing his access to the ghostly plane since he figured out Zig could pull him there when he was a teenager.

To us, when he went into the ghostly plane, it looked like he disappeared into thin air. Which tended to freak me out a bit sometimes, even though I was used to it. Seb always said I was too easy to panic with stuff like that—stuff I didn't know about or couldn't control—but he was just as bad as me.

"I heard that."

That made me sigh. *"Of course you did."*

"You're thinking awfully loudly over there today, A."

"Sorry."

"What the hell? Why are you apologizing? You never apologize."

"I apologize."

"Yeah, after I practically force you to."

I sighed again. *"Not true."*

"Wow. Just... just wow." He eyed me for a moment. *"Are you sure you're feeling alright?"*

I flipped him off, and he gave my hand a light smack, chuckling. Hearing that sound made me crack a smile and helped ease a little of the tension in my chest.

"Are you two done with your telepathic argument yet?" Del asked, bringing my attention back to him and his men.

I lifted a brow. "How do you know we were arguing?"

"When are you *not* arguing?"

"We don't argue *that* much," Seb said, looking totally affronted. That made me smile too.

"Riiiiiight." Del exaggerated the word. "You two *never* argue."

Seb waved him off, and I said, "Okay, you little turd, we get it."

He chuckled, and I was glad for it since I could tell he was being hard on himself.

Getting back on task, I asked, "You can't follow the life essence from the ghostly plane?"

Del shook his head. "Unfortunately, no."

"Damn. I was hoping you'd be able to see it from there."

"Sorry."

I glanced at my kid, then walked closer and placed my hand on his shoulder, giving it a squeeze. "Kiddo, you don't have anything to be sorry about." He went to open his mouth, and I was sure he was going to apologize again, so I cut him off. "Nope. Nothing at all. Thank you for looking into it. Pops and I will have another go at it. Don't worry, alright?"

He stared at me for a moment, then sighed and ran his hand through his hair. He wore it braided back on one side the same way I did, only his hair was blond. After a moment, he said, "I can't tell what kind of creature did this, but the magic feels similar to fae magic."

I released him and stared for a beat. "So you think we're looking for a creature that originates from Faela?"

Many of the magical creatures we had here came from there. But so many of them had come here centuries ago and were now considered natural inhabitants of Brinnswick.

"That's what I'm thinking. I know that doesn't narrow it down a whole lot—"

"But it's a start." I sent him a smile, then reached out with my magic to inspect the objects. I let my magic seep in around the mistletoe that immediately started going crazy when it felt my energy.

I focused on the magic, trying to get a feel for who or what put a curse on this little monster decoration. Just like before, I couldn't even tell what type of creature it was. But I could sense exactly what Del meant.

It really did feel similar to fae magic. Sort of earthy and otherworldly. Faela had so much magic it was almost overwhelming. It was distinct and very different from my magic, even though my magic was nature-based. The fae were made of Faela magic themselves, and their magic felt almost like Faela itself, so it was hard to distinguish the two. I'd visited Faela so often I was surprised I hadn't picked up on it sooner.

"It really does feel similar to fae magic."

"Agreed."

"Good catch. Thank you, Del."

He nodded. "You're welcome. Sorry I wasn't more hel—"

"You were plenty helpful. Stop apologizing." I looked at Nik and Gray. "I think it's time for you two to drill it into his head that he's helped us a lot, and everything he did is enough."

Nik nodded, and Gray smiled, saying, "Don't worry, we will."

I pulled Del into a hug and whispered, "I mean it, Del. You did great. I'm proud of you, and I appreciate your help. Thank you."

He was quiet for a beat before he gave me an extra squeeze. "You're welcome."

I released him, kissed his temple, and let him go so Seb could hug him again. Then I walked over to Nik and Gray, and without a word, I pulled them each into a hug, silently apologizing for my shitty mood when I'd come in. Since they both hugged and smiled at me, I figured I was forgiven.

Seb and I collected all of the spelled Christmas objects—and my viramore graciously carried the shield-enclosed doll so I didn't have to get close to it—and we headed back to our house.

"Straight to the basement," Seb said as we walked in through the back door.

"Lead the way, baby." Once we were down there, I headed to the work table we had set up on the side of the large room. The basement was filled with rows and rows of shelves, and nearly all of them were filled with dangerous magical items. We also had a vault built into one wall with even more precautions and wards set around it for the really, really dangerous shit.

And inside that vault was a large chest with the stuff that really shouldn't exist. The stuff we had no idea how to destroy—the stuff of nightmares.

We didn't mess with things in that chest.

Ever.

We set the stuff down, and I backed up, staring at it. All the pieces were encircled by a shield, and all the damn things were wiggling around, smacking into the shields, and trying to bite and claw their way out. It was kinda creepy, if I was being honest.

Especially that damn doll that didn't look any better at all now that the blood on its face had dried. I held in a shudder. So gross.

I stepped up to the mistletoe, ready to examine it with my magic again, but Seb moved into my path, blocking me.

I raised an eyebrow. "Can I help you?"

"Yes. Come upstairs with me."

I opened my mouth because that sounded like an amazing idea, but then the moving teddy bear caught my eye, and I grimaced. "As much as I want to take you up on that offer, I need to figure this out."

He shook his head. "Not tonight, you don't. We're not going to figure anything new out tonight."

"But maybe if I use more magic or... something..." I... wasn't confident that would work.

"You know that won't work."

"But—"

"We're going upstairs, eating some leftovers, then going to bed."

"But—"

"Ailin."

I sighed. "Sebastian?"

"We need to get some sleep so we can come at this from a new angle. We got maybe two hours last night. We're not thinking clearly. We're tired and starving, and I really just want to hold you for a little while before we have another hectic day tomorrow."

That made me soften a bit. He wanted to hold me for a little while? I... really liked the sound of that. "Okay."

He opened his mouth, clearly ready to argue with me some more when he realized what I'd said and snapped it shut.

I laughed and kissed his chin. "Let's go eat, cuddle, and sleep."

He opened his mouth again, then snapped it shut and gave me a nod, waving at the staircase. "I mean, if you don't want to hear the rest of my arguments, lead the way."

I headed for the stairs. "You're dying to get them out, aren't you?"

"No."

I laughed. "You liar."

He sighed, then smacked my ass. "Shut it, A, and move faster."

With a chuckle, I reached the stairs and walked out of the basement, doing my best to leave work down there so I could enjoy my viramore for a little while.

He was right. We weren't going to get anything productive done tonight on so little sleep. We needed food and rest.

And cuddling with my viramore sounded like the best damn idea yet.

Chapter Eight

Ailin

I didn't realize how hungry I was until Seb set a plate of food in front of me and I inhaled the smell, making my stomach growl. The second I ate a bite, it was like my stomach came alive, and the next thing I knew, I'd eaten every single thing on my plate and was getting up for seconds.

Seb seemed amused by this, but he didn't complain that he had to wait for me to finish my second plateful. As soon as I was finished and we had our dishes cleaned, dried, and put away, my viramore grabbed my hand, led me to the staircase—we both toed off our shoes and kicked them toward the front door—up the stairs, and straight into our bedroom.

I knew he had plans to simply put me to bed and cuddle up behind me so we could get a good night's sleep, but the food had given me a little boost, and we actually had the night to ourselves for once. It was such a rare occurrence, we had to take advantage of it.

So as soon as he shut our bedroom door, I pushed his back against it, leaned into him, and captured his mouth. He moaned and grabbed onto me, kissing me back with just as much passion.

I felt my magic flare, and his answered without hesitation, bursting out of him and reaching for my magic. The blue and green swirled around us, and I smiled against my viramore's lips.

He mumbled, "God, I love you, Ailin."

My heart leapt at that. He could tell me he loved me five million times, and it would still leap every single time. "I love you too, baby. So fucking much."

He groaned, grabbed hold of my hips, and turned us, pushing me against the door this time. Keeping his lips on mine, he unhooked my arm bracers and threw them on the floor before pushing my shirt up. Apparently, he was even more impatient than I was—I was all for it.

We only parted for a second while he pulled my shirt over my head and dropped it on the ground. Then he went for my pants, and I realized he was going to have me buck naked in a second flat, and he'd still be completely clothed.

Sometimes I liked that, but not right now. Right now, I needed to feel him, skin to skin, against me. I wanted to run my fingers all over him, feel his soft skin and hard muscles, and definitely the little softness he now had around his belly—we both had that these days. And I knew Seb was sometimes self-conscious of his, but I truly loved it.

It was sexy as hell because it was him, my Seb. It was sexy as hell because we weren't young anymore, and that small change only proved how long we'd been together, that we were growing old together—slowly, yes, thanks to magic, but still growing *together*.

And right now, I wanted—needed—to see all of him.

So I reached for his arm bracers and undid them quickly while he pushed my pants and underwear over my hips. Because he started bending over when I was messing with his bracer, I accidentally elbowed him in the chin.

"Holy shit, I'm so sorry."

He laughed. "It's fine, sweetheart."

Gently, I gripped his chin in my hand and forced him to meet my eyes. "Did I hurt you?"

He smiled at me and kissed the tips of my fingers. "Not even a little bit."

I breathed a sigh of relief because I could feel the truth of his words.

He kissed my palm. "Worrywart."

I grunted and couldn't even deny it, then decided to kiss his smirk away and leaned in to do just that. When I pressed forward and deepened our kiss, Seb hummed—I loved that sound—and kissed me back just as deeply.

When I broke the kiss, he groaned and reached for me, but I gave him a peck and whispered, "Take off your shirt."

He did it without question, and I finished taking off my pants and socks. As soon as Seb had his shirt off, I unhooked his pants and started pushing them and his boxer briefs off, too impatient to wait any longer.

I ran my hands over the soft skin of his hips and moaned in approval, then leaned in and kissed his belly before licking a stripe up his chest and over to one pec. Sucking on his nipple elicited a moan from him, and I hummed in approval. Then I kissed my way along his collarbone and up his throat, giving him a little nibble. I didn't leave a mark, but I knew exactly what spots to tease to make him moan and groan and whimper, and I couldn't help but smile against his skin when he let out those sweet sounds.

His hands skimmed the skin of my arms, my shoulders, and my back until he reached down and squeezed my ass. When his pants hit the floor, I leaned back up to kiss him again. He kissed me back with so much passion, so much love and desire that my chest warmed with pleasure and my magic sped up its dance as my cock hardened further.

"I want you, A," he murmured against my lips.

"You have me—all of me, whenever you want."

He made an unintelligible sound and gripped my ass harder before releasing one cheek. I felt him call on his magic, and I knew exactly what he was doing... the lube spell. I was all for that idea.

When his finger brushed over my hole a minute later, it was covered in lube. I fucking loved that we didn't have to interrupt ourselves to go find some. *Lube spell for the win.*

He pressed his finger inside me, and I groaned as I ran my hands over his biceps and shoulders. He kissed down along my neck, and I leaned my head back against the door, giving him more access.

When he added a second finger, I gripped his hair and lifted his head back up to me, demanding another kiss. Mother of All, I loved his mouth on mine, his larger body caging me in, his talented fingers making me want to tell him to forget the prep and get the hell inside me.

My hips moved against him, making my dick rub against his, then taking his fingers farther in, over and over again. *Fuck.* It felt so good, but it wasn't enough. I needed more of him.

"Seb." It sounded like I was whining. Or maybe like I was begging.

"I got you." He pressed a hard kiss to my lips.

Finally, he pulled his fingers out of my ass, grabbed my hips, and turned me around. I didn't hesitate to spread my legs and brace myself against the door. Seb brushed a kiss against my neck, lined himself up, and pushed his hips forward. I pushed back, trying to take him faster, but his hands on my hips slowed me down.

And that made me groan in frustration. He always did this to me.

He chuckled and kissed my neck. "That's because I refuse to hurt you."

"You won't."

"Mhm." He ignored me completely and kept at his slow-ass pace, trying to torture me to death. "I'm not trying to torture you to death."

"The laugh in your voice states otherwise." My voice came out breathy and ended on a moan when he pushed farther in. Oh fuck. Fuck, fuck, fuck, so close. "Come on, Sebastian."

He kissed my neck. "Patience, Ailin." He kissed my neck again. "We'll get there."

I made an unintelligible sound as he pushed forward again.

But then finally, *finally* he was fully seated, and I blew out a breath, willing my muscles to relax as my viramore continued pressing sweet kisses to my skin and our magics swirled around us.

"Please move," I whispered when I was ready, and since he could feel my truthfulness—and my eagerness—he didn't hesitate to slowly pull almost all the way out, then press back in just as slowly.

"Torturer."

He chuckled. "You like it."

All I could do was grunt—half from annoyance, half from pleasure.

I rested my forehead against the door with my eyes closed as he ever so slightly started to increase his speed. By the time he was slamming into me, I felt like I was going to explode.

Seb reached around my body and took hold of my cock, pumping it in time with his thrusts. The dual sensations sent sparks through my belly, and before I could stop it, my orgasm rushed through me.

I saw white, and I swore it was like sparks were flying around us.

Seb could feel my euphoria through our viramore bond, so he was only a beat behind me, coming in my ass as he shouted and trembled with pleasure.

"Oh fuck," he moaned out as his forehead fell onto the back of my neck.

I groaned in response and reached back with one arm to grab hold of him. I could only reach his hip, but that was fine because I could feel him everywhere.

My pleasure was his pleasure, and his was mine, echoing back and forth and extending it on and on. And with that pleasure came such a huge rush of love it was overwhelming. My own love and affection for him reflected back, making warmth bloom in both our chests. Our magics were mixed so thoroughly you couldn't tell them apart, and feeling them together was like the sweet icing on top of the delicious cake.

All of that together intensified everything, electrifying every inch of my body and soul. The pleasure went on and on and on, so long I didn't think I could take anymore.

When it was finally over, I felt wrung out, like my body was made of jello. I was pretty sure I would've fallen to the floor if Seb hadn't been holding me up.

We stayed there, breathing hard for a few minutes with Seb kissing my shoulder every now and then and holding me tight to him. I leaned back against him with one arm over his, holding on while I calmed down. Both our magics were slowly twirling around the room, calming along with us.

Once I'd gained my breath, I used my magic to clean us up—sometimes I truly loved my magic—then I lifted Seb's hand from around my waist and kissed his palm. He gave me a squeeze and wordlessly pulled me over to the bed.

My viramore sat me down, gently pushed on my chest until I lay down, and covered me up. Then he walked around to the other side of the bed, crawled in, and pulled me into his arms so he was spooning me.

"I've been dying to hold you all day," he muttered as he got comfortable.

That made me smile. I wiggled back into him until I was in the perfect spot, then I pushed my ass back against his cock and whispered, "And it's perfect for morning sex."

He snorted and shook his head. "You're ridiculous."

"Just wanted to throw it out there in case you wanna take advantage."

He smacked my hip lightly. "How are you not... you know... sated right now?"

I laughed. "That pained you to say out loud, didn't it?"

He sighed. "Yeah, yeah, it did."

That made me snort, and I wiggled into him a bit more. "I am *sated* as you put it. That was... fantastic."

He hummed and kissed the spot behind my ear. "I thought so."

I lifted his hand so I could kiss his palm again. "I love you, my viramore."

"I love you too, sweetheart."

I smiled and twisted until he gave me a kiss, then we both settled down for sleep.

I was just nodding off when our bedroom door opened, and I tensed until I realized Seb had opened it with his magic for our Bonded. I was so close to sleep that I hadn't noticed them asking to get in. *Whoops.* That was what happened when Seb was so attentive and knew exactly how to sate me. The two of them trotted in, hopped on the bed, and settled on top of our pillows.

Sera nuzzled my hair, and I smiled as I slipped into sleep, safe, sated, and loved.

Chapter Nine

Seb

Ailin was still in my arms when I woke up, and I couldn't help but tighten my hold on him and nuzzle into the back of his neck even though he was still asleep. I placed a kiss on his skin and breathed him in, content to lie here like this and let him get some much-needed rest.

The man did *not* get enough sleep. He was always rushing off to help someone, whether it was taking care of bad guys or simply helping one of the kids with something around the house or even babysitting.

I mean, I was right by his side every step of the way. But he tended to take everything on and carry it like he was solely responsible for saving everyone and keeping every person in our family safe and happy—hell, most of the time, he felt responsible for every single person in Brinnswick, period.

He wanted to help people. All. The. Time.

Simply put, he was a good guy. A fantastic guy.

And I was certainly lucky to have him.

But he was prone to worrying, despite the attitude he sometimes put off to other people.

I felt the moment Ailin woke up, and he let out a soft hum, kissed my palm, and settled into me, so I kissed his neck again.

"Can we just stay here all day?" he mumbled.

"I wish." I glanced at the clock on the nightstand and made a face. "We should probably get up... but I want to hold you for a while longer."

"I like that plan." He gave my arm a squeeze, and I could tell he was happy to doze for a bit.

It was unusual for him to want to lie in bed when there was an open case going on, so I was all for taking advantage of this while I could. I didn't know why he wanted the extra cuddle time, but I'd take it.

I kissed his neck and shoulder every now and then and buried my nose in his hair.

"I probably stink," he muttered a while later, more awake now.

"Only a little bit."

He laughed and tried to pull away, but I didn't let him. "If I stink, let me go."

"Nope." I kissed his neck. "I'm just as bad as you are, so it really doesn't matter." I gave him another kiss. "Also, I was kidding." Another kiss.

He sighed and started to twist to face me, then aborted the movement and pushed back into me again. "I was going to kiss you, but I know how you are with morning breath."

"As much as I want to kiss you too, I'd rather wait till we brush our teeth."

He waved me away. "Yeah, yeah."

We stayed there for another few minutes before I whispered, "Ailin?"

"Yeah, baby?"

"You feeling okay?"

He exhaled loudly. "Yeah, I just...don't want to face the day."

I took a moment to rifle through his emotions to figure out why he didn't want to face the day. When I finally figured it out, I wanted to shake the man. "Ailin, for fuck's sake." I sounded exasperated because I was. "It's not your fault we can't find the perp."

"I should be able to figure out what kind of magic's on those toys. I should be able to follow the life essence to the perp. I should be able to—"

"No." I said it loudly and sternly, cutting him off. "You are not some all-knowing entity. You're not infallible, as much as that fucking sucks. You're still just a person like everyone else. No one else has been able to figure those things out either. If I can't figure it out, and all our kids—who're all powerful in their own right—can't figure it out, why do you think you should? I'm sorry, sweetheart, but sometimes you're just as human as the rest of us."

"I'm not human."

I sighed. "You know exactly what I mean by that, and I'm *so* glad *that* is all you took away from what I said. Thanks."

He tapped my hand. "It's not all I took away. I... I understand what you're saying—hell, I even agree with you. But that doesn't really make my... emotions about the situation any better."

I gave him a squeeze. "I get it, but you need to give yourself some grace."

"I know I do. I'm trying."

"That's all I ask." I kissed his shoulder again.

"Thanks, Seb."

I kissed his neck. "Anytime. Are you ready to get up now?"

"I guess. But you have to promise me one thing."

"What's that?"

"After we finish this case, we're doing a naked weekend."

I snorted. "What the hell's a naked weekend?"

"I mean, it's kinda obvious, right? We'll be naked... for a whole fucking weekend."

I couldn't help but chuckle at that. "Honey, that's never going to work. Our kids are in and out of the house too much."

He pushed his ass against my groin. "But I like this."

"Of course you do. Tell you what, after the case is done, we can do a naked picnic in bed as a date and stay naked all night... in our room."

God, when we'd first started dating, there was no way in hell I could've ever imagined those words coming out of my mouth. Even now, after being with Ailin for a lifetime, I could feel my cheeks heating with embarrassment. Which was ridiculous.

He huffed. "Fine. You draw a hard bargain."

I snorted and smacked his ass. "Come on, sweetheart. Let's get up and get ready." Time to face the music.

After we showered and got ready, we sat at the kitchen island, eating breakfast when Ailin's phone rang. He picked it up and put it on speaker, saying to me, "It's Bas."

I gave a nod and looked down at the phone lying between us on the counter. When Ailin didn't say anything, I said, "Hey, Bas. Everything okay?"

He sighed, long, drawn-out, and exhausted-sounding. *"There are more attacks happening right now. Another neighborhood on the other side of town. So far, this one seems to be smaller than the last attack, but we need more people able to destroy the toys. As of right now, it's only toys this time, but who the hell knows if that'll change."*

"Send us the location, and we'll head over there now."

"Sounds good. Thank you." Bas hung up, and a text came through a few seconds later.

I stood and stretched. "Well, looks like we're in for another long day."

"Looks like."

We grabbed our phones, wallets, keys, and Bondeds and headed out.

W e arrived at the address Bas gave us, and I sighed as we got out of the car. There was another temporary base tent down the street, and as expected, there were a ton of people milling about with BCA jackets on and toys all over the ground, most of them burnt to a crisp.

Before we could make it to the tent, Basil and Hiro caught up to us, and Bas said, "We already took care of all the houses on this street, but there are a couple on the next street over with more calls coming in. Will you guys help us there?"

"Sure thing." I nodded at him. "Lead the way."

We followed the two of them down the road, waving at Alec along the way so he knew we were here. Bas pointed us to a house, and we headed in while he and his viramore took another one. Hiro might not have been a witch, but he was a hell of a good fighter, and the two of them worked really well together. They tended to take on the toughest cases brought to the BCA, and they always handled them well—and they knew when to bring in backup.

Which meant I wasn't really worried about them against these damn cursed toys. I mean, Bas was our kid, Hiro was our son-in-law, they were our family, so there was always some worry, but it was way less than it'd be if some of our other kids were running headlong into danger.

This house turned out to be much of the same as the other night. There were four toys attacking with teeth and claws. When we captured the little spelled objects, cleared the house, and took them outside, Ailin said, "Let's keep these to compare them to the other day's. At some point, this guy has to make a mistake, right?"

I sure as shit hope so.

We kept them in shields, and I checked my phone.

Alec had sent us a list of addresses, and I sighed. How was this happening to so many people? How had someone snuck by us so easily and created an attack this widespread? Where did they come from?

We went through several more houses—I honestly lost count—and ran into some of our other kids. Thayer and Toby were taking on houses together, and Clover and Jorah were working together since their viramores didn't like working for the BCA. And of course, we saw Basil and Hiro off and on.

We were getting to the end of our list and about to enter a new house when we heard someone yelling outside. Ailin and I didn't hesitate to rush over, and when we saw it was Jorah who was upset, we sped up even more.

Jorah used his Three power to open up a portal—it looked like he literally ripped open the air—and he stepped through before we could reach him. Clover stepped in after him.

"Jorah!" Ailin yelled, but Jor didn't hear him.

Luckily, Basil and Hiro came running out of one of the houses, and our kid called to us, "There's an attack at the school! The decorations are attacking kids. Jor and Thay are already going." Then he too used the Three magic to open a portal, only he didn't disappear right away and waved us over. "Come on!"

Jorah, Thayer, and Basil could speak telepathically to one another because of their Three magic, so it wasn't surprising that Bas knew what was going on.

But fuck. The school? No wonder Jorah and Thayer had left without us. Jorah had two kids still in that school—Nerissa, a sixteen-year-old mermaid shifter, and Raif, a thirteen-year-old satyr. And Thayer and Toby's only child—Safa, a sixteen-year-old witch—also went there.

Fuck, fuck, fuck.

I could feel Ailin's panic with a large dose of anger thrown in.

No one attacked our grandchildren.

No one.

Ailin and I both walked through the portal without hesitation, and Hiro and Bas came in behind us.

Since the Three magic was linked to Faela—the land of the fae—in order to travel anywhere, Jorah, Thayer, and Basil had to open a portal into Faela. Once in Faela, they could open a new portal to anywhere in our realm.

We'd traveled this way many times over the years, so I wasn't surprised when we landed in a world of pink. Like... absolutely everything was pink—the trees, the flowers, the grass, the flying bug thing that looked kinda cute but could probably eat me in one bite, the house that our kids owned here, the bunny-looking thing with six ears that could also probably eat me, absolutely everything was pink.

One thing I'd learned quickly was that no one could go around touching *anything* while in the land of the fae because nearly everything had secret teeth that could and would bite. Even animals that looked cute, or maybe *especially* animals that looked cute, had a way of luring a person in just to open their mouth wider than what looked possible—all animals were dripping with magic here—and take a bite out of them.

Unfortunately, I'd seen way too many things turn into scary creatures here, so no matter how cute something looked, I stayed far, far away.

And made sure all my grandkids stayed far away too when they visited.

It was like a blast of pink to the face, but Basil was moving quickly, so I didn't have more than ten seconds to take it in before he opened up a new portal and waved us in.

We landed in front of our grandkids' school. The school was open to anyone, even humans, but it had a large focus on magic and learning to use your power, so I wasn't sure a human would even want to go there.

It was the same school our kids went to, the same school Ailin attended. I didn't go here because I grew up thinking I was human, and back then, the supernatural community was in hiding, so I didn't even know magic existed, let alone that I was a member of the supernatural community. I thought it was all make-believe. Like all the fairytales I'd read growing up were just someone's imagination gone wild.

When I was a kid and young adult, I never would've believed magic was real without seeing it with my own eyes.

But this school had existed, even back then, and it had grown enormously over the years. It was a great school that Ailin and I both loved for all our kids and grandkids.

But right now, this place was even more chaotic than the street had been two nights ago. There were children *everywhere* and a ton of adults, including the police and a bunch of teachers. Everyone looked frazzled, some people were crying, and there were still kids and teachers running out of the building.

I spotted Toby, Thayer, Jorah, Clover, and Laiken—Jorah must've stopped at his house to pick up his viramore before coming here—heading into the school.

I pointed at them. "Over there!"

Ailin followed my gesture, then took off at a run.

A cop tried to stop him, but I yelled, "He's Ailin Ellwood." I hastily grabbed my BCA badge—Alec had given them to us for exactly this reason since not all officers recognized us on sight—and held it up to him. Ailin was already halfway to the door. "I'm Sebastian Ellwood. We're here to help."

The guy's mouth moved up and down like he was in shock, but I didn't have time for that, so I took off after my viramore, stuffing the badge back into my pocket as Zammerra held on to my shoulder for dear life.

When I crossed the threshold, I grimaced as I took everything in. A very long piece of garland hung from the ceiling, going nuts and trying to bite everything that passed by.

Luckily, it was already under a green shield. Not Ailin's. I could sense magic and recognize my viramore's and my family's. So after feeling it, I knew it was Jorah's magic. He had nature magic like Ailin, so it looked almost identical to the untrained eye.

Bells and bows and Christmas balls and other ornaments hung off the walls, and all of it was trying to eat kids as they ran past. There were even a few on the floor, rolling after children with teeth chomping away.

My viramore and our kids were already trapping all the decorations inside shields. But I saw a rogue bow sort of jumping along the floor, so I called on my magic and wrapped that sucker up in a shield.

Then I rushed over to catch up with Ailin and the kids.

"Where are they?" I asked, not needing to say I meant the children. Zamm growled from my shoulder, adding her own concern into the conversation.

"I don't know," Thayer said, burying his fingers in his hair. "I can't find them. Where the fuck are they?"

Jorah shook his head. "I don't know. I can't... I... fuck, I can't find them either. What if they—" He sucked in a breath, cutting himself off as his eyes welled with tears.

My heart sank, and my chest felt heavy as I realized what he meant.

What if our grandkids were hurt? Or... or worse?

Chapter Ten

Ailin

"Jorah," I said, placing my hands on Jor's shoulders and forcing him to look at me. "Close your eyes, take a breath, and reach with your magic. You'll be able to sense them. They're your kids. Thay, do the same thing, please."

All of their kids might've been adopted, but they absolutely still held the same parent-child bond that they would if they were blood related. Much the same way I had a bond with all of my kids.

Toby held onto his viramore while Thay reached out with his magic. And I kept Jorah calm. Seb threw a shield over the top of our group, keeping us safe and keeping watch while I took care of our son.

Yellow—from Thayer—and green—from Jor—magic floated around us, and I prayed that it would find the kids, that they were alright.

Please let them be okay. Mother of All, please.

Jorah sucked in a breath. "I got them. All three of 'em. They're in the back of the school. Holy shit. They're okay."

Thayer said, "I feel them too. Oh, thank the Mother."

Jor opened his eyes. "Thanks, Dad."

"Anytime." I nodded, and from her perch on my shoulder, Sera me-owed, just as relieved as I was that the kids were alright. "Now, let's get those kids."

"We need to shield the monsters and the kids as we go, guys, or we'll get overrun on our way back out," Seb said. *"Plus, the other kids need our help too."*

I overheard his thought and rolled my eyes at him. "Obviously." Then I turned around and threw a shield over the top of three kids who'd come out of a classroom and got cornered by a rogue Christmas wreath. "Stay there. My shield will keep you safe, okay? Nothing can get to you."

While I was taking care of the kids, Seb threw a shield over the top of the wreath. We sure did make a good team.

"Holy shit," one of the teens said. "That's Ailin Ellwood."

"You're safe."

The kid gave me a wide-eyed nod.

I gave them a two-finger salute, then shot Seb a small smile before charging down the hallway.

In my head, I overheard Seb say, *"My viramore is a force of nature, that's for sure."*

I snorted at that and continued on my way.

A Christmas ball came rolling out of a classroom, and since I was feeling especially stabby, I threw an energy ball at the damn thing, blasting it to pieces.

"Shit, A, be careful. Don't destroy the school," Seb said, staying by my side and elbowing me.

"I don't give a shit about anything but getting our kids out."

"And keeping the other kids safe too," Seb added, and I had to nod in agreement because, yes, I wanted that too, and he obviously knew it. As if either of us would ever let other kids get hurt.

Jorah pushed to the front of our group, clearly impatient. "Follow me."

We ran through the hallways, and as we went, we put shields over the top of groups of children—we even checked the classrooms—and shielded all of the Christmas monsters we could find.

Finally, we reached the back of the building where the gym was. The doors were closed, but Jorah burst through with Laiken, Thayer, and Toby behind him. Seb and I were right there as well.

I sighed in relief when I saw all three kids—along with at least ten others—already under a shield of their own. One of my grandkids had covered the entire group with a shield, and it made my heart happy to see her protecting so many people. Relief rushed through my entire body.

They were okay. They were safe—well, relatively safe—and we were going to keep it that way.

"Oh, thank fuck," Seb breathed out. "They're okay."

His relief matched my own, making tension leave both our bodies.

I examined the group of kids quickly, making sure I didn't see any dire injuries, but I didn't see even a drop of blood. That didn't mean that no one was injured at all, but at least I knew it wasn't an emergency.

Toby used his vampire speed to rush across the gymnasium to the kids, and his daughter, Safa, opened her shield for him. She closed it as her dad nearly crashed into her, pulling her into a huge bear hug. I couldn't blame him for reacting like that. If I had vampire speed, I would've done the same thing.

Thayer, Jorah, and Laiken all ran over quickly, and Safa let them into her shield before she extended it to cover Seb and me. That was sweet and cute, and honestly, amusing to have my granddaughter shielding me.

Seb looked over at me and winked, and I could feel his own amusement at the situation. It made me shoot him a small smile. Both of us were beyond reassured and hella proud of our granddaughter.

Both Sera and Zamm hopped down from our shoulders and trotted over to the kids, slinking in and out of them, rubbing on them, and checking them over while offering comfort.

I took in the entire gym to check for any monsters, and my eyebrows rose as I saw a large chunk of garland under its own shield, plus three other decorations all under one as well.

And every single one of them was Safa's shield. Impressive.

"She's getting stronger every day." Seb's voice was loud and clear in my head.

"Hell yeah, she is. Look at that."

"I know."

"We've got a little badass on our hands."

He shot me a smirk before heading closer to our grandkids.

Safa had been doing extra training with her dads and with me because she decided she wanted to go into the BCA when she grew up, just like her dads. So I shouldn't have been surprised. But practicing fighting moves and magic with your family and actually doing it out in the field under stress and panic were two vastly different things.

Not only had she acted under pressure, she'd kept her cousins and classmates safe.

And I had to assume that my three grandkids found each other in the chaos before shielding themselves because I knew Raif wasn't in any of the girls' classes since he was three years younger.

"I'm really proud of you," I said as I finally got a turn hugging Safa.

"Thanks, Granddad."

I smiled, gave her an extra squeeze, then pulled away, keeping my hands on her shoulders. "You did real good, kiddo."

She grinned at me. "This is what you've been training me for, right?"

I nodded. "Are you hurt?"

"I'm fine."

"What happened?"

Seb had finished hugging our other two grandkids, and he moved closer so he could hear what Safa had to say.

"When things started attacking people, the principal told everyone over the loudspeaker to get out of the building, but it was clear that a lot of kids were having trouble finding an exit that wasn't blocked by a monster. So Nerissa and I decided to go find Raif before we escaped. I used my magic to push the monsters away—I tried to blast them, but I remember Dads telling me about the attacks from the other night and how they caught the monsters instead so they didn't damage property. So I decided to do that too. I caught a couple of Christmas ornaments in that hallway." She nodded to a different door than the one we'd come through.

Wow. She really was a total badass already, and she was only sixteen.

She continued, "That's where Raif's classes are, so that's where we found him. He had a couple of friends with him, so Nerissa and I thought it'd be good to take them along too. Then we heard screaming in the gym, and I couldn't just leave whoever it was, so... we came in here, and I didn't think I could protect this many if we were on the move, so... we waited. I knew you guys would show up soon." She shot me a smile.

I pulled her back into a hug. "You did the right thing. You did so good, kiddo, so fucking good."

She let out a small laugh and pulled away. "Thanks." Before she could say anything else, my viramore had her in his arms, whispering things to her.

I walked over to Nerissa next and pulled the young mermaid into a hug, whispering, "Good job finding your brother and all three of you sticking together."

"Thanks, Granddad. I'm glad Safa was here to shield us."

"Me too." Mother of All was I glad for it. "Are you hurt?"

"No. I'm fine. Safa kept me safe the entire time."

I sent her a soft smile and kissed her temple. Next, I pulled Raif into my arms. "Thanks for staying with your sister and cousin."

He snorted. "I wasn't running out of here without them."

That made me smile. Raif was a satyr, so I wasn't sure he could do much against the Christmas monsters, but it was a sweet sentiment. Although, he could probably use his strong hoofs to stomp on them in his satyr form... but I was glad he hadn't tried it. It wasn't worth the risk.

After kissing the side of his head and releasing him, I asked, "Any injuries?"

"Nope. I'm good."

I nodded at him, then looked at the other kids. "Is anyone injured?"

There were shakes of their heads, but one teenager pointed at his friend and said, "I think Abel broke his ankle."

"I'm fine," the kid, assumedly Abel, said.

"No, you're not." The first kid glared at him.

Laiken rushed over to the kids, saying, "I've got it, Ailin. I'll let you know if we need help."

"Thanks, Laiken."

That worked well for me because I needed to clear the rest of the building and make sure no one else was hurt or trapped.

I caught Seb's eye, and he gave a nod of understanding.

We walked to the edge of Safa's shield, and I asked, "Can you hold your shield for a while longer, Safa? We need to clear the rest of the building."

She rolled her eyes. "Haven't I been practicing holding a shield for hours while you fling magic at me?"

Okay, true. "Fair enough. But are you sure—"

"I'm fine." She opened her shield for us.

Seb and I walked out, and I wasn't surprised when Basil, Hiro, Jorah, Clover, and Toby came out as well. Laiken and Thayer—along with both my and Seb's Bondeds—would stay behind to guard our kids and take care of the whole group. Plus, leaving our Bondeds behind meant we could use our bond with them to pull ourselves back here in the blink of an eye, and our Bondeds could do the same if we needed their help. I'd take any extra protection I could get when it came to keeping our grandkids safe.

We all walked out of the gym and went in different directions to cover more of the school. All of them could hold their own, especially against the Christmas monsters, so I wasn't worried about them going off in pairs or groups of three.

It didn't take long before the only place left in the school that no one had cleared was the auditorium. We ran into Bas and Hiro, and they decided to join us. We found a handful of monsters on the stage, and just as we were heading into the seating area, Jorah, Clover, and Toby came in to help as well.

Since Bas, Jorah, and Thayer could speak telepathically, it wasn't surprising that Jorah had been able to lead Toby, Clover, and himself into the auditorium where we were.

"Laiken and Thayer are leading the kids out of the building now," Jorah said. "Since the gym's so far away and the doors are even farther from here, I told them it was safe to take them out."

"Sounds good. I'm sure the teachers and parents outside are worried about their kids," Seb said.

I hummed in agreement. It would probably be good for the kids to get away from the monsters, not because they were dangerous—since they were trapped—but for their mental health. I couldn't imagine having decorations attack them with teeth and claws was anything but a nightmare for most kids.

I headed down another row of auditorium chairs. We went through each and every one, just to be safe. As I reached the end of my row, something jumped out from under one of the chairs and latched itself onto my leg. My leg bracers kept me from feeling its teeth and claws, but I still hopped out into the main aisle so I could actually see what the hell was attacking me.

When I glanced down, I grimaced. It was a Santa Claus statue kind of thing, but it looked more like a... like a doll. A Santa doll.

I shook my leg vigorously, trying to get the damn thing off as my heart raced. The second I stopped shaking out my leg, the thing's head turned and looked right up at me.

I let out an involuntary scream and started hopping around and shaking my leg, yelling, "Get it off me! Seb! Get it off me!" My viramore was already running toward me, but that didn't stop me from screaming at him, "Hurry the fuck up! Get it off me!"

Without hesitation, the second Seb was close enough, he reached down, grabbed the thing's little body, and yanked it off me. He had it trapped in a shield a second later.

I looked down at it and made a disgusted sound of surprise when I found it already looking at me. "Mother of All, get that fucking thing away from me."

Seb, very obviously trying not to laugh, said, "Sure thing, sweetheart."

He used his magic to push his shield up the aisle, and when it passed by me, I let out another sound that was definitely *not* a scream, no matter what Seb said.

I backed away quickly as Seb's magic took the gross Santa doll-statue thing with it.

I shuddered as I watched it go. What the fuck? What the actual fuck was even going on right now? *Fucking hell.*

Seb turned to me, and it was extremely obvious that he was hiding a grin. "Are you okay?"

"Yes. No. I mean, yes. I'm not hurt." I huffed, and my viramore let out a small laugh.

Seb covered his mouth, like that could hide the fact that he was laughing at me.

But then I realized I could hear other laughter. No, not just regular laughter, *hysterical* laughter. Slowly, I turned around and found my kids cracking the hell up.

Jorah pointed at me, then wiped tears from his eyes, and the little shit laughed out, "I've never... seen you... freak out... like that. Holy shit... hilarious."

Basil, still laughing, said, "Funniest thing... I've *ever* seen. Fuck, I'm gonna... be laughing at this... forever."

I flipped them both off, but all that did was send them into another fit of hysterics.

And then a bubble of laughter came from right beside me. I turned a glare on my viramore even as I felt amusement at myself fill my chest—not that I was going to let anyone else know.

He stared at me for a beat, then a full-on laugh burst out of him, and he bent in half, laughing so hard he couldn't even stand up, apparently.

With one hand resting on his knee, he lifted the other at me in a placating gesture. "I'm sorry... I just... oh my god... Ailin." He laughed for a full thirty seconds before trying again. "I'm sorry. I... you... oh my god."

Since that was all he was capable of saying, I sighed and ignored him, then turned to walk down another row of seats.

Basil called over, "You sure you wanna do that? There might be another Santa under there." He started laughing before he finished speaking, but I still understood him.

Seb, Jorah, Hiro, and Toby all laughed with him.

"Fuck you all." I flipped them off again, and they cracked up.

But then I eyed the row, and a bit of anxiety made my chest clench. What if there really was another Santa in there? What if it jumped out and *looked at me*?

I shivered involuntarily. *Fuck.*

Seb, still chuckling a tiny bit but at least able to walk, moved closer and kissed my cheek. Then through our bond, he said, *"Why don't you start ushering all the monsters out of the school? You can start destroying the things outside. The kids and I will finish in here."*

I frowned at him. I knew he was only offering because he knew I was nervous—not scared, never scared—of running into another Santa, or Mother forbid, an actual motherfucking doll.

Okay, I was actually freaking scared. And I knew that was so fucking ridiculous, but holy shit, those things were creepy.

To Seb, I asked, *"You don't mind?"*

"Not at all." He gave my cheek another kiss, then gave me a small push toward the door. "Go."

I sighed, annoyed at myself more than anything. "Thanks."

Since my kids laughed again when they realized I was leaving, I flipped them off as I walked out the door, then snorted in amusement when they laughed harder.

Then I got to work, pulling all the shielded monsters along with me—not even glancing at the gross Santa.

By the time I made it outside, I had more monsters than I could count, and it made me clench my teeth. Someone had done this.

At a school.

To children.

Who in the fuck messed with children this way?

They'd messed with all those kids who'd only wanted a present from Santa. Then they messed with all the kids at the houses today. And now this. A school. And not just any school, but my own grandkids' school.

Whoever had done this had endangered my grandkids.

My. Grandkids.

I ground my teeth.

The fucker behind this had no idea that he'd just sealed his own fate. Because if there was one thing everyone should know, it was that you didn't mess with the Ellwoods.

You didn't mess with my family.

Now, I was even more determined to find this bastard and take him down.

That asshole had no idea what was coming for him.

Chapter Eleven

Seb

Ailin was pissed, and honestly, I was right there with him. This had gone too far. It had gone on for too long.

We needed to find whoever was doing this and take them down.

"Yes, we really fucking do," Ailin said from the driver's seat beside me.

We were heading home with a few more Christmas monsters in our trunk, and we were planning on spending as much time as needed to find a fucking clue. And we *would* find one. No matter what it took.

When we parked, Sera and Zamm headed off so they could go for a flight together over the top of our coven land. They liked to patrol sometimes and keep an eye on our family's home.

Ailin and I went into our basement with our new haul. Then we each took one of the new monsters—I took a wreath, and he took some mistletoe—and we got to work.

I pulled on my magic, tugging deep into my soul, using as much power as I possibly could. My blue magic emitted out of me and surrounded the wreath I was examining. I took the shield down so my magic could touch the wreath itself. Then I put a new shield up around my magic and the wreath, but I kept the connection to the magic touching the wreath.

As my magic swirled around, I closed my eyes and tried to take in everything I could about the monstrous wreath and its magic. It felt the same as the monsters from the other night, but this time, it felt like there was more of it. Like the magic itself was more potent than the last time.

From beside me, I heard Ailin growl in frustration, and I turned to him, saying, "It's a little different than before, isn't it? More potent?"

My viramore sighed. "Yes, it is. But I still can't fucking follow it. How the fuck can we find this guy if we can't even follow the damn magic?"

I grimaced. "I'm not sure, sweetheart. We'll think of something."

"If you say so. I'm definitely not convinced."

I reached over and smacked his bicep. "Stop being so negative. Have a little faith in our abilities. We're not the only ones working on this. They have other BCA agents doing the same thing. Someone is bound to think of something."

"We're the people they call in when they have a magical problem they can't figure out. You really think the kids that work at the BCA are going to figure this out before us? I don't fucking think so."

I rolled my eyes. "You know... humility is a thing, right?"

He flipped me off. "I'm only stating facts."

Shaking my head in disbelief, I turned back to the monster I was examining. "Let's switch and see if we can figure something else out. See if all of them feel the same."

Surprisingly, he didn't complain about my request and easily switched out our monster objects. I did the same thing with the mistletoe as I had with the wreath, using my magic to examine it. It felt as potent as the wreath had. It felt the same as the others, like it was close to fae magic.

But as I went deeper into the mistletoe, I thought I maybe felt something a tad different than the wreath. Almost like it was made by a different person.

I opened my eyes and looked at Ailin. His eyes were closed, his brow was pinched, and he looked so freaking angry. It made me wince. He took things so personally, especially when something was aimed at a family member. Ailin's protectiveness knew no bounds.

As I examined him and his green magic, I watched it swirl around the wreath, and I suddenly had an idea.

"Ailin?"

He opened his eyes and quirked a brow. "Yeah?"

"I'm going to grab my staff, and then we're going to examine these things together. I know we tried combining our magic with the other monster objects already, but these guys are different. With their magic so much more potent, maybe we'll get lucky."

I stood up and headed up the stairs before he could respond. I kept my staff right by the front door because I often took it with me when we were going on cases. So I knew exactly where it was, and it took me no time to grab it and then rush back down to the basement.

"Okay, let's try this."

Ailin gave me a nod. "Go for it, baby."

Ailin and I both released our magics, and they didn't hesitate to swirl together between us. Our magics loved each other just as much as Ailin and I did, so whenever we let them out enough to play together, it was almost like they were eager to. That sounded weird and sorta like our magics were sentient, and maybe they were, to some degree, but I stopped asking questions about that a long time ago.

I closed my eyes and let my magic guide me. I could feel Ailin through our bond, through my magic, and all around me. It felt natural. It felt good. I loved when we combined ourselves in this way.

But unfortunately, it didn't bring any more clues to the forefront.

"Dammit," I growled out. "This is so fucking frustrating. I don't know what else to do."

Ailin looked helpless as he sat there, shaking his head and shrugging his shoulders. "I don't know either, baby." He sighed and dropped his face into his hands, rubbing at his eyes as he groaned.

I stared at him for a bit before a lightbulb went off. "What if we feed it some of our own life essence? Maybe if we have a connection to the life essence it's stealing, we'll be able to follow it."

He stared at me for a beat or two before blowing out a heavy breath. "Let's try it."

This time, I let Ailin take the lead. I'd been practicing magic for decades, so I was competent and completely comfortable in my ability. I could do things that many others couldn't, and I made sure to practice to keep myself sharp. But that being said, I didn't think I'd ever be at the level Ailin was at when it came to understanding how magic worked and being able to follow its components the way he could.

He probably wouldn't agree with me on that, but it was the truth.

"Why don't you let me feed it my life essence while you do the magic part?" I said.

He glared at me. "You really think I'm going to let you feed this thing your life essence? Have you lost your mind?"

I glared at him. "What the hell, Ailin? It'll be fine. I won't even feel it, for fuck's sake."

"I'm going to feed it *my* life essence."

"Ailin."

"Sebastian."

I stared at him for a few seconds before I let out a sigh. "Asshole."

He sent me a smirk before he reached over and touched the mistletoe. I flinched, even though I knew he wasn't going to get hurt. I still didn't like seeing it or seeing him take a risk like that. Which... was why he didn't want me to do it. He wanted to keep me safe as badly as I did him.

And, as usual, I let him get his way. The asshat.

I grumbled at the thought.

He sent me another smirk, as if he'd heard what I thought, and maybe he had. I was thinking pretty hard there for a second.

When he was ready, I tapped my staff on the ground and brought it to life, then pulled on its magic and sent it toward my viramore. Ailin latched onto it with ease, and I quickly added my own magic into the mix. The two of us stood there, staring at the crazed mistletoe while our magics surrounded it.

And then, by some miracle, I watched as a small glowing green orb rose out over the mistletoe and headed for the ceiling.

Holy shit. We could see his life essence.

Ailin and I exchanged a wide-eyed look before he quickly threw a shield around the mistletoe, picked it up, and ran for the stairs. I was only a step behind him, bringing my staff with me.

When we made it up into the dining room, I saw the little green glowing orb move straight through the front door.

"Holy shit," I said. "We really fucking did it."

Ailin was already rushing toward the door as he spoke. "We can't lose this thing."

"At least we know how to make it work if we do lose it."

Once I was through the door, I shut it behind me and ran down the porch steps, heading for our car. This thing was moving fast, and it wasn't going to move across roads, but I didn't think we had a chance of following it on foot.

I jumped into the driver's seat, started the car, and yelled, "Get in!" Then I closed my eyes and called on my bond with Zammerra. I asked her with my emotions if she would help us, then I sent her a mental picture of the green glowing orb I needed her to follow.

Her answering roar was felt through our link and physically because she wasn't too far from us. Through that roar, I knew she was saying that she and Sera would follow the orb for us.

I blew out a relieved breath as Ailin hopped in, and I took off, heading out of our property.

"Zamm and Sera are following it."

"Good. I have the mistletoe in case we need to do it again, but hopefully, they won't lose it." Ailin threw said mistletoe in the backseat. I could hear the thing wiggling around in its shield, and I wrinkled my nose.

How long did this curse last? Were these cursed objects meant to just... remain little monsters until someone blew it to smithereens? Or would the curse's effects fade after a certain amount of time? Or perhaps after it collected a certain amount of life essence?

Luckily, the orb floated just above the trees as we headed off of coven property and out of the Brinnswick Forest. Once we were on the street, it glided over houses and buildings with ease. Ailin rolled his window down and stuck half his body out to see where it went when we lost track of it.

I slapped his leg. "Get back in here. You're going to get hurt."

"We can't lose it, Seb. Turn right at the next street." I turned right, and he whooped. "I see it. Straight ahead for a little while."

"Would you get your ass back in the car? Zamm and Sera are on it. We aren't going to lose it, ass."

He huffed but finally sat back down in his seat. "Sorry. I just... this is the first time I feel like we're actually *doing* something, you know?"

"I know." I slapped his leg again, and he grabbed my hand, giving it a quick kiss before letting go and scooting forward in his seat to look out the front windshield.

Since I was driving, I only caught a glimpse of it every now and then, but I wasn't worried. Zamm would tell me where to go if need be.

We followed it for a little while, but I got caught at a red light, and by the time we got through it, we couldn't find the damn thing.

Ailin cursed. "Fuck! Dammit!"

"It's okay. We can just follow Zamm and Sera. Chill out, A."

He didn't say anything, so I concentrated on my Bonded, got a sense of where she was, and when the light turned green, I headed that way.

It took us about five minutes to catch back up, and I blew out a breath when Ailin said, "I see it."

Thank fuck. He was so anxious, it was making me anxious.

"Sorry, baby," A said after a minute. "I'm not trying to drive you up the wall."

"It's okay, I'm used to it."

He snorted and blindly smacked my chest, not taking his eyes off the orb.

"We're going to catch this guy, A."

He blew out a breath, trying to calm himself. "Hell yes, we are."

We followed the little bubble of Ailin's life essence down a few more streets and to the opposite side of the city from where the Brinnswick Forest treeline began.

When it floated into an old factory building, I was a little shocked. For some reason, I was picturing some kind of weird underground toy shop or something, not an ordinary-looking factory. But I guessed that made this operation blend in more. It looked so normal on the outside that no one would think twice or wonder if the owner was doing nefarious things.

I asked Zamm to shift to her smaller size and keep an eye on the factory from the roof of a building across the street while Ailin and I parked a few streets away. We weren't ready to go in, and the last thing we wanted to do was scare the bastard away.

Ailin went to get out of the car, but I grabbed his wrist to stop him. "We need to call in backup."

"Psh. We need to get in there right now before they leave."

I shook my head. "We have no idea what's waiting for us inside. There could be one man, there could be a hundred. We're not going in there alone without any backup, with no one knowing where we are, and without any kind of plan. I'm calling Alec. You need to call Basil. Get them here now."

He stared at me for a second. "I really want to get in there."

"And we will. Just not by ourselves. Okay?"

He stared again before blowing out a breath. "Fine. But I'm not happy about this."

I rolled my eyes. "Are you ever happy when it comes to working cases? Especially with other people?"

He flipped me off, and I chuckled, making him smile. And then, because I knew he was ready to burst, I leaned in and gave him a quick peck on the lips.

I closed my eyes and asked Zamm to show me what she could see, and when I got a vision of the building, I noticed a sign hanging over the front doors.

Merry Marketplace.

Well. That sounded like a holiday shop kind of thing, didn't it?

"Merry Marketplace," Ailin said, either seeing it through Sera's eyes or hearing my own thoughts about it. "Guess we're in the right place."

"Yep."

He sighed. "I'll call Bas."

I sent him a grateful smile, then pulled out my phone and dialed Alec.

We met Alec, our kids, and the rest of the BCA agents a few blocks away so we wouldn't be spotted, but Zamm and Sera kept their eyes on the building to make sure no one escaped before we had the chance to enter.

We made a plan with Alec, and he set everything into motion. He sent teams around to the back of the factory and the sides to surround the entire building so our perp had no chance of escape.

We were going for a frontal assault, and Basil, Jorah, Thayer, Clover, Hiro, and Toby were going in with us. The other agents would guard the outside to catch anyone escaping the premises.

"I'll go in first, Seb behind me, and you guys come in after him. Everyone, make sure you keep shields up as soon as you get into the building," Ailin said, completely taking over Alec's operation. His voice brokered no argument, and I was surprised that none of the kids—Basil especially—didn't try to argue anyway.

Even Alec didn't say a word once Ailin began giving everyone, not just our family, orders. I suppose Alec knew it was a losing battle when Ailin got like this.

Plus, no one could ever argue that Ailin didn't get results.

Everyone nodded their agreement, and then we all got into formation to follow my viramore into the building.

We moved quickly down the street and across the parking lot to the front door. Ailin wasted no time using his magic to unlock the door, open it, and put a shield up on the other side to keep himself and everyone else safe from any flying magic.

He stepped inside, and I was right behind him. But as soon as we cleared the doorway, I stepped up beside him and took in the large space.

My eyes widened, and I breathed out, "What the actual fuck?"

Chapter Twelve

Ailin

What the actual fuck?

Seriously. What the actual fuck?

I stared in astonishment, feeling like I walked onto a movie set or something.

In the middle of the room there was a large conveyor belt with a ton of Christmas decorations being moved along it. At the end of the belt, there were a bunch of delivery boxes.

And all around the belt and boxes were a shit-ton of... elves.

Little guys with pointy ears. They were even wearing Christmas colors with little hats on their heads.

Was I... hallucinating or something?

I blinked.

Nope, they were still there.

But... this couldn't be real, right?

Christmas elves... weren't a real thing, were they?

I rubbed my eyes.

And nope, they were still there.

What in the ever-loving fuck is this?

"What the fuck is this?" Seb asked in a hushed voice. "Santa's Evil Workshop?"

I opened my mouth to respond, but I honestly had no words for him. It was easy for me to read the magic the elves were using, so it was clear to me that they were cursing each of the decorations or toys that passed over the conveyor belt, then packing them up into boxes and sending them on their way.

Santa's evil workshop, indeed.

After a few seconds, I nodded. "It looks like it."

All the elves were staring at us with terrified expressions, and I didn't know why, but I just couldn't imagine them at the heart of this horror-fest of Christmas decor. Maybe their small statures, rosy cheeks, button noses, huge eyes, and cuteness were getting to me, but seriously, I couldn't believe they were cursing toys for kids and decorations for people who celebrated Christmas. That was ridiculous.

Elves were generally good guys, weren't they? They didn't have a mean bone in their bodies, did they?

But... just because I'd known some good elves in the past didn't mean all elves were good. That was just dumb. All types of creatures had good and evil among them.

I had so many spells floating around me, ready to attack and take down the baddies, but these guys were just... standing there. They weren't running. They weren't attacking. They didn't even look like they were ready to defend themselves against me.

I dropped my spells because I didn't want to scare them more than they already were.

Which was... unfair after everything they'd done to people the past few days. They sort of deserved to be terrified, didn't they?

I heard Seb's voice in my head say, *"They don't feel evil. What the hell?"*

"I don't know, baby."

Alec said, "Let's get these guys in restraints or shields so we can clear the building and interview them."

"Right."

Seb and I—and all of our kids—began throwing shields over the top of each and every elf. There were so many that we had to group them under the shields, but that was fine since they couldn't escape.

Not that they seemed inclined to.

Not a single one of them tried to run from us, not even when it was clear we were apprehending them.

Most of them were hunched into themselves or holding onto other elves for comfort. They looked as if we were the bad guys who'd come in to destroy them all.

If they were so bold as to curse so many things and send them off into the world, why the hell were they cowering now? What the fuck was going on?

These were not the evil criminals we were expecting to find.

While we grouped the elves together and moved them all to one side of the factory, other BCA agents cleared the rest of the building, coming up empty.

Toby and Hiro worked together to clear the office that was on an upper level, overlooking the conveyor belt, and Hiro called down to me, "Ailin, you might wanna come up 'ere. There's lots of paperwork, so you might find somethin'."

"Thanks, Hiro," Seb said for me, and I gave our son-in-law a nod.

So once all the elves were secure, I headed up there to search the place. Seb came with me, and the two of us started rifling through the many, many books and papers that were strewn about. Honestly, it looked like it'd been ransacked before we'd even gotten here.

"This is... weird." Seb sighed and rubbed his face.

"Weird how?" I picked up another piece of paper and sighed because it was a water bill and was addressed to Merry Marketplace. There wasn't an actual name anywhere. Everything was addressed to the business, even the letters we found.

Very unhelpful.

Seb huffed out a frustrated breath. "Those... elves—are they really elves? I... I didn't think tiny elves like that existed. I've never seen them before."

"They're elves." I discarded yet another piece of useless paper. "I've only seen them one other time when I was a kid, and my dad told me that most elves like to stay in Faela. Something about the way our magic here feels against their skin or something—I can't remember. But anyway, yeah. They're elves, but I'm not surprised you haven't seen them before. They're rare here, and I'm not sure if there are any living on the Pink Isle either."

The Pink Isle was the island we always visited when we went to Faela, the land of the fae. Hence all the pink when we traveled through Basil's portal.

Seb scratched his nose, meeting my eyes. "Hm. So that makes this even stranger. They're so rare, don't like being here, and yet, they attack everyone? That just... doesn't seem right. I don't feel like I'm getting anything malicious from them."

I sighed. "I don't either. But, Seb, you saw what they were doing, right? They were putting curses on the decorations on the conveyor belt. We literally caught them red-handed."

He made a noncommittal noise and glanced through the window down to the floor where all the elves were.

I glanced down as well and frowned. Now some of the elves were crying.

For fuck's sake, I wasn't supposed to feel sorry for the damn creatures that'd been terrorizing the city for days.

Fuck.

My nostrils flared, and I went back to digging through paperwork.

Seb kissed my cheek randomly as he walked past me, and it made me smile a tiny bit. He was so sweet, and the fact that he'd done that while we were at work was pretty rare. He *hated* public displays of affection when we were working. He always maintained this *we're at work and need to be professional* attitude. Which I got, but sometimes it was fun messing with him.

The fact that he'd kissed my cheek while we were in the middle of a case in some random factory, working with a ton of other BCA agents was possibly a sign that he wanted something.

"What do you want?"

Seb looked at me with raised eyebrows. "What do you mean?"

I huffed. "You just willingly did some PDA *at work*, so... what do you want?"

"I wanted to kiss your cheek, that's all."

"I don't believe you."

He rolled his eyes. "You can believe anything you want, but that doesn't change the truth."

I narrowed my eyes at him. "You want something."

He looked at the ceiling and let out the most dramatic exasperated breath I'd ever heard. "God forbid I do something nice."

"Hm."

"Ailin Talamh Ellwood, if I wanted something, I'd simply tell you. Why the hell would I need to kiss your cheek first, you weirdo?"

I shrugged. "Dunno. That's why I'm asking you."

"I don't want anything."

"Sure you don't."

"Oh my god. Ailin."

"Mother of All. Sebastian."

He narrowed his eyes at me. "I just wanted to kiss your cheek."

"Uh-huh."

He let out a frustrated growl. "For fuck's sake, A."

I couldn't help it, I grinned.

His eyes narrowed. "What the hell? Were you messing with me?"

"I had to find something fun to do while we went through paperwork hell."

He flipped me off and turned away, ignoring me.

A small laugh came out, and I walked over to him and wrapped my arms around his shoulders from behind since he was sitting. I kissed the top of his head. "I love you."

He grunted.

"I love you so, so much."

He grunted again.

"I love you more than anything else in the world."

He stayed silent.

I almost snorted at the stubborn man. "I love you so much, I think I'm going to hug you for the rest of the day. You won't be able to go anywhere without me right on your ass."

"You fucking will not be doing that."

I laughed and bent down to kiss his temple.

He sighed, long and loud and dramatic. "I love you too."

I snorted, gave him one more head kiss, and released him before turning back to the desk.

A few minutes later, Alec appeared at the door with his hands on his hips, looking irritated. "Can you come talk to the elves? I need someone that can try different languages. I asked them a few questions, and they stared at me like I had three heads."

"Sure." I put the papers I was holding down. "There isn't anything in this office anyway."

He sighed. "Figures. I'll have a few techs come take a look as well."

I gave him a nod and followed him out the door. Seb came with us, probably because he was curious about these elves and why they'd turned this place into Santa's Evil Workshop.

All of the little guys were now gathered in a group and underneath one large shield, so I supposed we were doing a group interview first. We'd have to do individual ones back at the BCA headquarters.

I stood in front of the group, staring at them for a long minute before I asked, "Why the hell are you cursing things and sending them to unsuspecting families?" When I got no response, I repeated the question in Fae'lee, which I figured they spoke.

All of them looked even more terrified than when I first came over. They were exchanging glances with each other and huddling closer to one another. It took over thirty seconds for one brave elf with big green eyes and brown hair to come forward and speak in Fae'lee. "We have no choice, sir."

My brow furrowed at that. That sounded like a bullshit excuse if I ever heard one.

"Maybe you should give them the benefit of the doubt," Seb said through our bond.

I glanced at him. *"Really? You're buying this bullshit?"*

He shrugged and ran his teeth over his bottom lip. *"Honestly, I kinda am. I told you before that I don't sense any malice from them, and that still stands.*" He waited a beat, and when I didn't respond, he added, *"At least hear them out."*

I grumbled under my breath. *"Fine."* Out loud, I asked in Fae'lee, "Why? What's forcing you to do this?"

The elf bit his lip, his huge eyes darting between Seb, Alec, and me. It took a long time for him to answer. "Our master."

It took a few seconds for that to sink in, and when it did, I wanted to explode. "Who's your master? Where is he?" The elf shrank back, and I realized I'd growled the words out and my magic was angrily whipping around me. More calmly, I said, "No one's going to hurt you, okay? But I need you to tell me who your master is. Please."

He shook his head. "Can't say."

"Please. We'll help you get away from him."

"Can't say... want to, but can't."

I stared at him for a beat and tried my best to rein in my anger. I wasn't angry at the elves; it wasn't their fault. I was angry at whoever had enslaved them. I wanted to ring that person's neck.

"Can you tell me your name?"

He nodded. "Rilitar Shacan."

I knew Alec would already have people looking up the guy now that we had at least one name. Hopefully the rest would be as easy to get.

To the elf, I said, "I'm Ailin Ellwood, and this is my viramore, Sebastian Ellwood."

He nodded and put his hand over his heart in a greeting of respect. Huh.

"Are you under a compulsion?" I asked the little guy.

He opened his mouth to speak, but nothing came out, and when he tried to talk a second time, he started gagging. He grabbed his throat and bent over, trying to catch his breath.

Shit. Clearly the compulsion or spell wouldn't allow him to talk about it.

I grimaced and was going to ask Basil to let me through his shield to help, but a few of the other elves helped the poor guy.

After they made sure he was okay, another elf with bright blue eyes and blonde hair came forward and said, "We can't help you. We're sorry." She looked terrified of my response.

"It's okay. I'm going to figure this out. What's your name?"

"Nimeroni Aratris, sir."

"Nice to meet you. I'm Ailin." I turned to Seb. *"You were right."*

"Wow. You're even admitting it."

I rolled my eyes and grunted.

"Told you. Thanks for hearing them out, A."

I waved that off and looked back at all the little elves, then cringed as I thought of something. "Is this master going to come after you when he realizes we stopped your little setup here?"

Nimeroni winced. "Yes. He won't let us go easily."

I turned to Alec. "What the hell are we going to do with them? They're in danger. We need a safe place to take them." To Seb, I added, *"And who the fuck is behind this? How are we here, and we still don't have a fucking answer?"*

"I don't know, but we're closer to one, right? We... we have to be."

I sure as shit hoped so.

Chapter Thirteen

Seb

Ailin was going to bring the elves home with us, I just knew it.

When my viramore turned back to me, I could already see the question in his eyes, so I spoke before he could. "No. Absolutely not."

"But, Seb, what if the bastard comes for them? Who's going to protect them?"

I crossed my arms over my chest. "What if the bastard forces them to attack us in our sleep?"

"I don't think he can control them from afar like that, especially through our wards. I think he has to give them a vocal command."

"And I think that you don't know that for sure, so they *could* attack us. Or, you know, anyone in our family."

He fully faced me, crossing his arms over his chest and mirroring my stance. "Then we put them in our shed with blankets and air mattresses or whatever, and we can build a shield around the entire building. They won't be able to escape our shield, no matter what compulsions they're under."

"Ailin."

"Sebastian."

I glared at him, then turned to look down at the little elves. Most of them were watching our exchange, looking afraid and vulnerable. And cute. And sweet. Those little button noses were adorable. They were so tiny, it sorta made me want to pick one up and carry it around in my pocket or something.

Dammit!

I turned back to my viramore and blew out a long, slow breath. "*Fine. But they're not coming in my car, Ailin. I mean it!*"

He smirked at me and leaned in to brush a kiss across my jaw. "Whatever you say, baby."

"Asshole," I muttered under my breath.

I glanced in my rearview mirror and sighed. There were probably twenty elves in my backseat right now and several sitting on Ailin's lap beside me.

The rest were in Alec's car behind us.

Because of course my asshole viramore had won that argument too. Of fucking course he had.

Had Ailin ever *not* been able to convince me of something?

Nope. Not a once.

"You're such an asshole."

I was facing forward, but I saw him turn toward me. "Me? That was so random. What did I do?"

My eyebrows shot up into my hairline. "Really? You *really* have no clue what you've done?"

"Uh, no."

"Ailin! Are you fucking kidding me? What the hell? Take a look in the fucking backseat, you asshat!"

He started laughing and reached over to pat my thigh. "I'm joking, baby. Relax."

I grunted and murmured under my breath, "How the hell am I supposed to relax with a fucking elf party going on in the backseat?"

But I did take a deep breath, trying to bring on the calm. At least they weren't as bad as the damn beasties he made me drive around a couple of months ago. I swore it felt like he had me drive creatures around every few weeks. Why I even bothered to tell him they weren't coming into my car, I didn't know.

As if he'd suddenly start listening to me now after fifty years, I had no idea.

I'd gone through several cars in that time, and every single one of them had suffered the same fate—becoming a supernatural taxi service.

Ailin chatted with the elves on his lap, and the ones in the back spoke quietly to one another. Sera was in the middle of the backseat with a bunch of them crawling all over her. Zamm decided she wanted nothing to do with them and curled up around my neck. I suppose we were the sourpuss twins at the moment.

With that in mind, I did my best to let go of my annoyance. It wasn't the elves' fault they were in this situation, and if I was being honest, I wouldn't want them to be anywhere else since I knew we could keep them safe.

By the time we got to the border of our coven land—where our wards started—I was much calmer. I slowed the vehicle down to a stop, then looked over at Ailin, who shot me a small smile.

"Alright, guys," he said in Fae'lee. "I need to add you to my wards so you can cross over into our territory."

For some animal-like species, our wards allowed them free range, but it seemed that the elves were a little too high on the magic scale for them to cross without our aid.

Ailin called on his magic, and I watched the green swirl around the car, encompassing each and every elf. His magic swirled through the windows and out the back toward Alec's car where I knew it was wrapping around the rest of the elves.

Then I watched it race forward and hit an invisible wall. The green crashed into it, and because I was now good at wards, thanks to Ailin, and because I was connected to this particular ward, I could see a sort of ripple go through it.

From right in front of us, the ripple shot out, flying to either side of us and up and up and up. Our wards went high into the sky, giving our dragons and other flying beasties plenty of room to stretch their wings without worry of an attack.

I would've thought the whole thing excessive except for the fact that we'd been attacked so many times throughout our lives that I'd lost count, and we'd been in a few wars and lots of battles as well. Knowing what kind of monsters were out there made me appreciate our wards more than Ailin knew.

I didn't think we could be too careful when it came to protecting our homes and family members.

Ailin recalled his magic and opened his eyes. "Done."

I gave him a nod, then slowly pulled forward into our long driveway. I felt the moment we crossed over. It was like moving through jello. It was hard to breathe because the air was so damn thick with magic, but the sensation was over after only a few seconds.

The elves all made sounds of surprise as they passed through, but no one had any trouble, so I knew Ailin's magic had done its job.

I drove up to the house and couldn't help but smile at the awed sounds coming from the little guys. I could understand the amazement. The first time I saw Ailin's house, I thought I'd hit my head and fallen into a fairytale. I mean, who in the world would've thought that someone could ask the trees to form into a house like that... and that the trees would remain living. Living and happy, if Ailin had anything to say about it, and he did.

Our home was beautiful and looked like something out of a dream. It was literally a few gigantic trees that Ailin had asked to grow into a house with rooms, doors, and windows. There were branches coming off it that had gorgeous green leaves in the spring and summer, but right now, they were bare. It honestly looked like someone had built it to look like a real tree, but no. It was living because Ailin's magic was amazing.

I parked the car at the top of the driveway, unlocked the doors, and got out, then opened the back door for the elves. They tumbled out, taking everything in with wide eyes on their little faces.

Alec parked his car behind ours—he'd have to drive it out of the driveaway, go down the road, and pull into his and Aspen's own driveway later—and the elves from his car looked much the same—in awe.

Ailin said, "The shed is this way. We don't really use it much, except to store chairs, tables, and our movie projector, so hopefully, there'll be enough room for you guys."

"Ailin?"

He stopped in his tracks to face me. "Yeah?"

"I'm going to go find all our air mattresses and extra blankets and pillows."

"I can help after I show them the shed."

I waved him off. "It's fine, sweetheart."

He nodded, but I could tell he was hiding a small smile. "Thank you."

After the kids moved out, we started using all their old closets as storage space, and since we had a million kids and grandkids, we needed all the pillows and blankets we could get for any impromptu sleepovers.

I went inside and headed up the stairs to one of the spare rooms where we kept our air mattresses. We had at least three or four of them, but I didn't think more than two would fit in the shed. Two might be pushing it.

As I hauled the second one out, Alec showed up in the doorway, saying, "I'll take those if you want to find the blankets and whatever else you guys are giving them."

"Thanks, Alec."

He smiled and picked up the heavy-ass things as if he was picking up feathers, showing off his werewolf strength. Either that or I was a lot weaker than I thought. Which was... definitely a possibility.

I went into yet another spare bedroom for the sheets and blankets, then another one for the pillows. By the time I was heading outside, I had a giant mountain of fluffy things in my arms. It was so high, it was taller than my head, so I was walking as carefully as I possibly could.

"Mother of All, Seb, why didn't you call me or make two trips?" Ailin asked as he rushed over and took some of my load from me.

"I was fine."

He snorted. "Looks real fine to me. You're walking like two inches per step."

"I'll show you two inches."

He leaned in and waggled his eyebrows. "Oh yeah? I think I'd like more than two inches, if you're willing."

I laughed and elbowed him, shaking my head. "I swear you're like a twelve-year-old." I felt Ailin's magic move around me as I walked through the shield he'd already placed over the top of the shed. Since he was my viramore, and we were connected in every way, I could walk through his shields, and he mine, without us having to open them or allow passage like he'd had to do for the elves with the property ward. One of the many benefits of being soulmates.

"It made you laugh, so I guess that makes us both twelve."

"Nah. I'm at least thirteen."

He snorted at that and opened the shed door. When I walked in, I stopped mid-step, and my eyes widened.

I didn't know what I was expecting, but it certainly wasn't Alec bent over, trying to get the air mattress air pump to work with three elves on his back, another elf swinging from the rafters in the short ceiling, four elves stacked on top of each other's shoulders, trying to reach a shelf, at least seven elves jumping on the air mattress that was already blown up, and five or six of them running around in a circle in the middle of the room, screaming like banshees.

"What in the fuck is happening?" I asked.

"No idea. They weren't like this when I left, and I was only gone for like one minute tops."

I grunted.

"How... how did they do all of this in that short amount of time?"

I shared a wide-eyed stare with Ailin before I set my bundle on the air mattress that was already blown up and slowly backed toward the door.

"I'm... gonna go make dinner. I'll bring out some food for"—I waved in the general direction of... the entire elven troupe—"everyone when it's done." No idea what the hell I was going to make that would feed this many people, but I'd figure it out.

"Don't leave me," Ailin said.

"You'll be fine."

He glared. "Just gimme a second, and I'll come with you."

"Just come in when you're done."

"Please wait for me." His face was so grumpy it was cute.

I sighed. "Fine."

Ailin loudly yelled in Fae'lee, "Everyone! Seb and I are going to make you some dinner. We'll be back in a little while. Do you need anything else before we leave?"

The female from earlier—Nimeroni—stood up straight from where she perched on Alec's back. "We're okay, sir. Thank you."

"Alright." Ailin gave her a long look. "Please don't hurt yourselves. Or Alec."

"We won't, sir," she said, just as another elf went swinging by, yelling, "Weeeeeee." Where he got that rope, I'd never know.

I winced when the little guy let go of the rope, flipped in the air, and landed on the pile of blankets I'd set down. That was far too dangerous for my liking.

Oh boy. I needed to get out of here before I started yelling and ruined all of their fun. I was sure they wanted to celebrate being away from their tormentor, and I didn't want to get in the way of that.

So I tugged on Ailin's sleeve to get him moving. Luckily, he followed me, and I called over my shoulder, "Come eat dinner with us, Al. Call Aspen to join us."

"I will," he answered, finally getting the air pump to work.

I didn't want to be here when he tried to get the elves off his back so he could stand up straight.

As soon as we were inside our house with the door shut tight, I said, "What the hell did you bring home this time, Ailin Talamh Ellwood?"

He sighed and rubbed the bridge of his nose. "Honestly? I have no idea."

I let out a dry laugh as I aimed for the kitchen. "Lovely. Come on, let's figure out dinner."

Almost as soon as I stepped into the kitchen, Ailin grabbed my hips and turned me around to face him. He stepped closer with his hands on the small of my back and pulled me in so we were hip to hip.

He met my eyes. "You're amazing."

I snorted. "Yeah, okay."

He gave me a little shake. "Hey, you *are* amazing. You just helped me save an entire troupe of elves."

I rolled my eyes. "Yeah, only because you begged me to."

"Sebastian, stop being difficult and take a damn compliment once in a while."

I sighed and wrapped my hands around his biceps. "Fine. You think I'm amazing. Thanks."

"Mother of All, you couldn't be more sarcastic if you tried."

That made me snort.

"You're amazing and beautiful and kind and sweet and so damn perfect for me you take my breath away."

"Okay, okay, already. If you're trying to get into my pants later, you've succeeded."

He chuckled. "That wasn't my plan, but I'll definitely take you up on that."

Ailin sent me a gentle smile, one that he only reserved for me and maybe the kids, then he leaned up. I met him halfway, leaning down to meet his lips with mine. He hummed against me and opened his mouth, and I took the invitation for what it was and brushed my tongue against his. This time, it was me who hummed in appreciation. I loved the way Ailin kissed me, the way he tasted, the way he felt in my arms.

His tongue swirled around mine before he sucked my bottom lip into his mouth, making me whimper. He pulled me tighter to him, and I reached up to bury my fingers in his hair. I had no problem with deepening the kiss even further.

"Oh, come on! Every fucking time!" a voice yelled. "Get a room, Dads!"

Ailin laughed, making me chuckle against his mouth before I sighed, broke our kiss, and rested our foreheads together for a brief moment. Ailin smiled at me, winked, pecked my lips, and stepped away, facing the intruder.

He said, "We have a whole house, actually." We ignored Basil's fake-gagging routine. "What's up?"

I peeked into the living room to see who all came in. Basil and Hiro were the only ones I saw. At least so far. I gave them a small wave and received smiles in return.

Basil sighed. "We haven't been home all week, so we're out of food. I was hoping we could come for dinner?"

"You know you're welcome anytime, Bas." Ailin walked over and pulled him into a dramatic bear hug. "This will always be your home, even if you don't live here anymore."

Bas looked a little flustered at all the emotions, so I wasn't surprised when he quickly released Ailin and stepped away. "Thanks, you old sap."

I chuckled at that while Ailin said with a laugh, "Little shit."

Bas gave him a big grin.

Just as I turned to walk back into the kitchen, I heard the back door open. Jorah, Laiken, and three of their kids walked in with them. The kids ran over and gave me quick hugs before heading for Ailin, and I wasn't surprised when he got pulled into playing a board game with them two seconds later.

Jorah moved over to me and asked, "Do you have room for more?"

I smiled at him. "Always."

He grinned, and for some reason, it reminded me of an Ailin shit-eating grin. "Good because Thay and Tob are right behind us."

I snorted at that. "Better get started then. I have an army to feed tonight."

"We'll help," Laiken said, walking into the kitchen as he rolled up his sleeves. "What are we cooking?"

"No idea. Maybe some kind of pasta since that feeds a lot."

"Alright, let's figure this out."

Laiken opened my refrigerator with pursed lips, clearly thinking, and it struck me how comfortable he, and all the kids, were in my and Ailin's home. None of them had a problem just coming in and going through our fridge and pantry. They were as comfortable here as they were in their own homes.

That thought warmed me more than anyone could ever know.

I loved that our kids and grandkids treated our home like their own. I loved that they enjoyed spending time with us. I loved that I was always surrounded by family. That they were all so loving and accepting of me and everyone we brought into the family.

I just... loved our family so much.

"And we all love you just as much, baby," Ailin said in my head, making me warm all over again.

"I love you too, A."

Chapter Fourteen

Ailin

The next morning, after saying goodbye to Opal and her viramore—they were staying at our home to do research—I walked out of the house with Seb behind me and came to an abrupt stop when a small voice said, "They're not taking over our land!"

Seb jumped in surprise and grabbed his chest, but he relaxed quickly before I even understood what the hell was going on.

It took me a solid twenty seconds to figure it out. Bramble Wrinkleblossom, an elder sprite that lived on my coven land after Seb and I convinced his clan to leave the human playground they'd taken over, was standing on my porch, yelling at me.

Sprites were *flower people* as Seb said, and Bramble looked like he was made out of sticks. His body was a long stick with stick arms and legs and leaves as wings. And being an elder and in charge of his clan, he'd somehow grown the top of his stick head into the shape of a crown. So he looked like a stick with two big leaves and a crown. He was usually quite sweet, but when he was concerned about something, he always came at us with anger and yelling.

"Um, hi, Bramble. What's up?" I was way too tired to deal with this right now.

He flew up to my face and hovered there. "You brought *elves* to our home, Sage! I won't stand for it. They're not taking our home from us."

"For fuck's sake, he's always so dramatic, isn't he?" Seb asked me privately.

"He really is." Out loud to the sprite, I said, "Of course they're not, Bramble. Do you really think I'd ever break my promise to you and your clan? I promised you safety here, did I not? I haven't broken my promise in the fifty years you've been here, and I don't plan on breaking it now."

He harrumphed.

I continued on. "I would never let anyone take your home from you. The elves won't go anywhere near your village. I can't promise that they won't stay because I haven't had that discussion with them, and I don't know if they have anywhere else to go. But I can promise that if they stay, they'll be sworn to keeping the peace of the land and all of its creatures, including you. They'll have to promise not to go on your territory without your say-so, alright?"

He stared at me for a long time, and I could tell he was still grumbling. Finally, he said, "Fine." He pointed his little bow at me—sprites made their own weapons and slathered them with a poison, so I really didn't want to get shot with one of his arrows. "But if they touch my land or my kin, I will end them."

I didn't want to promote violence between the two groups, but I wasn't about to start a whole new argument with the sprite. "Fair enough. Right now, they're stuck inside my shield, so you have nothing to worry about."

He harrumphed again and stomped his little stick foot in midair. "Fine. Make sure it stays that way."

"Will do."

I watched the little sprite fly off toward the two guards he'd left at the bottom of the porch steps. I was glad they hadn't come up on the porch because those two were a lot more trigger-happy than Bramble was, and the last thing Seb and I needed was getting shot by a sprite arrow. It would've knocked us out for hours—those things packed a punch.

Shaking off that encounter, I glanced at Seb. "Ready to go?"

"Yep. You drive."

"Yes, siree."

As we headed to the car, I glanced at the shed. Last night, I'd extended the shield to include a small area of grass so the elves could get some fresh air if they wanted. I felt bad trapping them in there like that, but with their torturer still on the loose, this was the safest way to not only protect my coven, but to protect the elves as well. If the person behind this was able to reach them from outside my coven's wards, there was still nothing he could do because the elves couldn't go anywhere. There was no way of getting through my shield, and the bastard couldn't reach them because there was no scenario where he'd be able to get through my coven's wards and onto coven land. None at all.

My land was the most well-protected in the entirety of Brinnswick, and likely, in the entire world. Although, I'd done an admirable job of ensuring my sons, Remi and Tan, who both lived in Gauhala, had fierce protections around them. And my grandson, Zaos, who lived out in another city in Brinnswick was protected just as well. But my coven land's wards were old, so the magic had been building for decades. My sons' and grandson's properties couldn't catch up time-wise, but they'd continue to grow in the same way.

So the elves were as safe as we could possibly make them.

We met at HQ with Alec and the rest of the BCA team that were on the mysterious Christmas decor attacks. Alec already had everything laid out in a conference room for us, and it didn't take long for everyone to get there.

Alec stood at the head of the table and clapped his hands once. When everyone settled, he spoke. "Okay, so we know how the guy was doing this—they forced a troupe of elves to curse the holiday stuff—but we don't know who this 'they' is or where they are. Hell, we don't even know what they are, other than assuming they're not human. I suppose they could be, but I have no idea what a human would do with all that life essence and fear energy."

Jorah lifted a finger in the air. "I have some ideas about that. The only creatures I can think of would be an incubus or a vampire."

"A vampire?" Bas asked. "What would a vamp do with all that energy?"

Toby broke in. "I've never done it myself, but I've been told that vampires can pull life essence into themselves. That's essentially what we do anyway, only we access it through blood. They call them energy vampires, for obvious reasons. I don't know exactly how it would be accomplished, but it's something to consider."

I tilted my head at him. "Do you know anyone older than you that we could ask?"

Toby stared at me for a beat, then shrugged. "Not really. I talked to Jules and Emrys last night, and neither of them know how to do it or know anyone that does. But I think you know someone, or at least, Bel and Tan do."

My brow furrowed at that, but Seb made an "ah" sound before saying, "Anton. He's ancient, according to Remi."

I stared at my viramore for a moment before smiling and giving him a nod. "That makes sense. Maybe we should give him a call and find out how likely that is. I do think the incubus guess is our best bet, but we'll have to double-check with Anton."

"I can call Remi and get him to connect me to Anton," Thayer offered.

Alec gave him a nod. "Do it."

Thay nodded, stood, and walked out of the room as he pulled out his phone.

"I think we need to consult our books," Jorah said. "There might be other creatures that can absorb life essence and fear energy."

I gave him a nod. "Actually, I already asked Opal and Laneo to take a look. They're going to grab Niya and her viramores too. One of them will give us a call if they find anything."

Jorah nodded. "Perfect."

I turned back to Alec. "Okay, so regardless of what he is, we need to know where he is more than anything."

Alec tilted his head to the side, like he was giving me a point. "True. But I'm stumped on how to find him."

"I... have an idea." I cringed a little because I knew this wasn't going to go well. Seb was going to hate it.

"Go on..."

"We set a trap."

When I said nothing else, Alec rolled his eyes. "That's all fine and good, Ailin, but what the hell would we use as bait?"

Here was the part Seb was going to hate. "The elves."

I felt Seb's anger, surprise, and concern through our bond.

Alec's eyebrows rose. "You'd let us do that?"

I wasn't surprised he'd asked that. For the past two decades, when I'd brought home a creature, I'd never let anyone use them as bait. That was the whole reason none of the others had suggested it before now. They knew—thought—I'd shut them down.

And normally, I would. But this wasn't a normal circumstance. This person was attacking people, attacking families, attacking kids, all over the city, and some of them were seriously injured. It was only a matter of time before someone was killed, and at the scale of these attacks, I was afraid it was going to be a lot of someones. They were going to wind up killing a lot of people, and we needed to stop them before they did.

I gave Alec a nod. "Yes. We need to ask the elves if they're okay with it, of course, but... yes, I think we should use them as bait."

"Ailin," Sebastian said, making me face him. "That's way too dangerous. You know this. It's why you've never let anyone be used for bait since..." He winced at that, and I sighed.

Someone had gotten hurt—they'd almost died—two decades ago by playing bait, and I'd shut that avenue down ever since.

There was no way I'd let a repeat of that incident happen again.

"I know, but we can keep them safe."

"How? If this person sees a shield around the elves, they'll just leave before we can catch them. If the elves aren't shielded, well, that's way too dangerous."

"We give them their own magically induced stick or whatever we can get that has a shield spell stored in it. Then we have our agents posted all around so we can give each other and the elves a warning when the guy comes on scene. I'll also be close to the elves so I can throw a shield around them if need be. We'll have multiple ways of protecting them."

"You really want to do this?"

I winced internally. "I don't *want* to do this, no. But I think it's our best, and really, our only option at the moment. The entire city's at risk because we have no clue how many boxes of cursed objects were already shipped. For fuck's sake, they could have an entire warehouse full of these things. And for all we know, these cursed objects have been shipped to other cities as well. We need to stop them."

He waited a moment. "We'll be right there?"

I nodded. "Yes. We can keep them safe."

Seb made a face at me like he wasn't so sure about that, then blew out an angry breath, faced the table with both elbows resting on it, and buried his face in his hands. I gave him a moment, and he eventually said, "Fine. I... see how that might work. I just... I don't want anyone getting hurt."

I set my hand on his forearm. "Do you really think I'm going to let any of those little elves get hurt?"

Without removing his hands from his head, he turned his head to meet my gaze. "No, I don't."

I gave him a small smile, leaned in to peck his lips, and faced Alec. "So... what do you think? Should we move on with the plan?"

"You're sure about this?"

"As sure as I can be."

He gave a reluctant nod. "Yes. Let's plan everything out, and when you get home tonight, you can talk to the elves. We'll plan for tomorrow, but you let us know if that changes after you speak with them."

"Will do."

Thayer came back into the room, holding his phone out toward the center, saying, "Alright, Anton, you have Alec, Ailin, Seb, Jorah, Clover, Basil, Hiro, Toby, and of course, me. Can you repeat what you told me about vampires sucking in life essence?"

"Of course," Anton's voice came through the phone, and Thay set it on the table. *"Hello, all."*

There was a chorus of greetings before Anton continued.

"They're called energy vampires. It's a rare skill, to be sure, but it is possible for a vampire to absorb life essence if it's pulled out of a person. It's something that takes a lot of skill and finesse, something that develops with age, so if you're looking at an energy vampire, they're sure to be hundreds of years old, if not older."

My eyebrows rose as I absorbed that, then I cleared my throat. "Do you know of any vampires in Brinnswick that can do this?"

Anton was quiet for a full minute. *"I... may know of a few possibilities, but no one in particular comes to mind. I don't know any vampires that prefer using that method rather than feeding. Feeding is much easier, especially these days when we can buy bagged blood or go to a vampire bar where there are always plenty of willing humans."*

That was true enough. There were plenty of people, especially humans, that sought out vampires, wanting to be fed on, some hoping to be turned themselves. Vampires weren't the scary monsters in the shadows anymore. They were out in the open, and plenty of people were fascinated with them.

Anton continued. *"But I can make you a list of possible candidates so you can check them out and eliminate them from your suspect pool."*

"That sounds perfect," Alec said. "Thank you, Anton. We appreciate your help."

"Of course. Please let me know if there's anything else I can assist you with."

"Will do. Thanks again."

Thayer grabbed his phone, took it off speaker, and put it to his ear, speaking quietly, before Anton could respond. He hung up quickly and retook his seat at the table.

Seb said, "I still think it's an incubus."

Bas shot him a grin. "Wanna take a bet? Incubus versus vampire?"

Seb snorted and waved him off. "Let's figure out exactly what we're doing tomorrow, yeah? We need to take every precaution to keep the elves safe."

The kids and Alec all agreed, but I didn't miss Thayer, Jorah, and Basil trying to get Hiro, Toby, and Clover to get in on the bet. Goofballs.

Right as we were leaving, another emergency call came in. More holiday toys and decorations were attacking people at a company holiday party in one of the high-rises downtown. It was a large business—an advertising firm or something—in a large building with lots of people.

The bastard must've had some boxes of cursed objects hidden somewhere else. That, or these things had already been shipped out before we'd shut down the factory yesterday. *Fuck.*

B y the time we got home, I was worn out... again. This had been another absolute mess when we'd arrived. We'd taken care of it, but now we were even more convinced that this incubus or vampire or whatever they were had a warehouse, or more than one, filled with more cursed objects.

Which meant we'd be getting even more calls like the one today.

We needed to sleep while we could so we'd be ready when we did.

But first, I had some elves I needed to talk to.

"Are you sure about this?" Seb asked me as we walked over to the elf shed.

"Yes. I think it's the best way to stop this guy."

He stopped me with a hand on my arm. "Are you sure we can keep them safe?"

I met his gaze. "Yes, baby. I'm sure."

He blew out a long breath. "Alright. Let's get these guys on board then."

Nimeroni saw us coming, and she came up to the edge of the shield. Since it would be awkward standing on the outside while she was inside it, I stepped through with Seb right behind me.

I smiled at the little elf who'd been more helpful than the others and spoke in Fae'lee. "I wanted to talk to you about catching the person who bound you."

I wasn't about to call that person their *master* like the poor elves had been saying because that was absolutely disgusting. No one should own another person, for fuck's sake. And yeah, elves were small, but that didn't mean they weren't intelligent creatures who deserved autonomy.

An expression of fear crossed Nimeroni's face, but she steeled herself and gave me a nod. "How can we help?"

Well, that was the perfect invitation, wasn't it?

Still, a bit of guilt crept in. I didn't want to make any of these elves face their torturer ever again. But did we have a choice?

I took a breath and went for it. "We need to capture this... person." It was incredibly frustrating that the elves couldn't tell us anything about the person who'd kept them captive. We didn't even know how long they'd been under the spell. "But the only way we know how to find them is... if he thinks he can get you back—he wouldn't be able to. We won't let him touch you or hurt you in any way, I promise. But... we kind of need some... bait." I cringed.

"That's definitely the way to get her to help us," Seb said in my head as he sighed out loud.

"Shut it, you."

He snorted in my head, managing to hide it on the outside.

And Nimeroni simply stared at me for the longest time.

It made me feel terribly guilty.

"We would only need a few of you to come with us, and we'll give you shield spells and other defensive magical items to keep yourselves protected. *And* Seb and I will be hiding right beside you. As soon as they show up, I'll put a shield over top of you all to keep you safe while the rest of the BCA close in on them and take them down."

She waited a few more seconds before she asked in a quiet, fearful voice, "You'll keep us safe?"

"I promise I will. You'll be my top priority."

"How many of us do you need?"

"I'm not sure. Maybe ten or so. We want him to detect where you are, and that will probably be easier if you're clustered in a group. We want you to keep your younglings and elders here and anyone else you don't want on the front line."

She gave a nod. "And after? You'll reunite us with our troupe?"

"Of course, Nimeroni. We don't want to take you away from your family."

"You promise we'll be together after?"

"Yes. I promise."

"And... you won't take over our spell?"

I blinked at that, surprised. She thought I was going to bind her people to myself? I was sure a look of horror crossed my face. "Absolutely not. I would never do that to you, to anyone."

She stared for a very long time before giving me a nod. "The sprite said you're trustworthy. That you both have good hearts. I believe him." She pointed at me with narrowed eyes. "But listen hard, Sage. If you keep us away from each other, we *will* find a way to destroy you. We will find each other again. We will stay together, no matter what."

"I would expect nothing else, Nimeroni. Thank you for helping us. You have no idea how much your trust means to me."

She took a breath, gave me a single nod, and turned on her heel. "I'll talk to my troupe. Tell you how many are coming."

"Thank you," I called to her back as she disappeared inside the shed.

Seb shook his head, staring after her. "I have no idea how you always get *everyone* to listen to you. It's like your superpower."

I snorted at that. "I don't have a superpower. Why would I need one when I have this?" I flashed my green magic, and that seemed to break the nervous tension Seb was carrying.

He snorted and shoulder-bumped me. "Show-off."

"That's me."

He chuckled again, and I couldn't help but smile with him, relieved for this small moment when so much was going on and stressing the both of us out.

Chapter Fifteen

Seb

In the end, Nimeroni was able to get ten other elves to stand in as bait with her. Among them was the other elf that'd spoken directly to us, Rilitar, and nine others I was still learning the names of.

And now, here we were, close to the factory we'd found the elves in, waiting for the big bad to show up. It was dark out—just in case it was a vampire who wouldn't be able to come out in the daylight—which was probably scaring the little elves even more.

This was it. We were locked in and ready to go.

I could only hope that we'd supplied the elves with enough shields and defensive magical items. There was an array of spells among them, but we'd made sure that each and every one of them had a shield spell, and a good one at that.

The eleven elves were standing around, eating a snack, trying to look natural but looking miserable and scared. Ailin and I were literally hiding behind a bush, although we had an invisibility shield over the top of us to help hide us. It wouldn't hide our magical signatures, but we were hoping the perp wouldn't notice until they were close and it was too late.

The other BCA agents, mainly our kids, were hiding in other spots around the elves. They were a little farther back since we were afraid the big baddie would be able to sense that many powerful people so close together, which meant Ailin and I were the elves first line of defense.

"My money's on it being an incubus," Ailin said to me through our link. We couldn't speak out loud without risking being overheard, so we were strictly speaking to each other through our bond.

We each had a little earpiece to keep in touch with the rest of the team, but no one was speaking out loud right now.

"I'm going with vampire."

"Why?"

"Because with it being an energy vampire or whatever, it's the weirder of the two, and you're involved."

He glanced at me with a raised brow. *"What's that supposed to mean?"*

"You always wind up with the weird and wild cases."

He went to respond, then ended up sighing and shoulder-bumping me. *"Fair."*

It took everything in me to hold in my snort of amusement. Opal and Laneo hadn't found any other possible creatures in our tomes at home, but they weren't finished looking through everything yet.

I was going to continue teasing Ailin, but I felt something in the air change.

Ailin obviously felt it too because he stilled and hyper-focused on the elves and the space around them. A van pulled up in front of the building, and every single elf tensed, shrunk in on themselves, and looked even more terrified than they had a moment ago, if such a thing was possible.

A tall man with blond hair, tanned skin, and an objectively handsome face stepped out of the car. Instantly, I could tell he was an incubus from the way he looked... almost too perfect or something. That and the fact that when his magic rushed over me, I could sense it.

The second he was out of his van, Ailin threw a shield over the group of elves. Then he stood and put one over top of the incubus.

Ailin had tattooed a rune onto my chest a long time ago that kept me safe from an incubus's thrall, so I wasn't too worried about facing one. He could reach out with his magic all he wanted to try and make me do his bidding, but it wouldn't work. Ailin had the same rune tattooed on his own chest, so he was safe.

Not to mention that the incubus was stuck under Ailin's shield.

The guy yelled and banged on the shield, but all I did was stare at him.

After a few seconds, I frowned at the creature and held in a sigh.

"What?"

"I'm... oddly disappointed that it's not something weird."

Ailin snorted out loud, and the two of us moved from behind the bush. Ailin walked up to the yelling incubus, and I walked over to the elves to make sure they were okay.

My Fae'lee wasn't nearly as good as Ailin's, but I could get by. "Are you all alright?"

Nimeroni nodded, then shook her head, confusing me.

"What's wrong? Is someone hurt?" I would've asked if someone was scared, but the obvious answer to that was that *all* of them were.

When she spoke, her gaze was on the incubus, but I knew she was talking to me. "That... that's not h—" Her voice cut off, and her face scrunched up in pain before she doubled over, grabbing her throat.

"Nimeroni!" I yelled before using my connection with Ailin to walk through his shield to get to her.

I knelt down and reached for her, but she was so tiny, I didn't know how to help without hurting her. One of the other elves grabbed hold of Nimeroni's shoulders and eased her back to standing after a few seconds.

She met my gaze, and I quietly asked, "Were you trying to tell me something about the compulsion?"

She made an aborted nodding motion, which was answer enough.

I thought about her words, trying to figure out what she'd been trying to say, but I didn't know. *"That's not h—"* That was all I'd gotten.

I glanced over at Ailin, who was looking pissed off and gorgeous as he tried to interrogate the incubus. Then I looked at Nimeroni again. At this point, we'd probably just have to wait until we were able to break the compulsion to find out what she wanted to tell us.

Nimeroni pointed at the incubus and shook her head for a second before that look of pain overtook her face again, and she bent over, grabbing her head. I went to help, but again, I didn't know what to do.

Since her friend was taking care of her, I looked at the incubus. What was she trying so desperately to tell me? Shaking her head no at him and, *"That's not h—"*

That's not h... hungry? Harry? Human? High, hair, hill, him, holly. Wait. Him.

My eyes widened. *That's not him.*

That's... not... him.

Holy fucking shit. Was that right?

I looked at the incubus, then at Nimeroni, then back again.

That's not him.

"That's not him," I whispered to myself. With a sudden jolt, I jumped to my feet and yelled to Ailin, "That's not him!"

My viramore turned in my direction, but before we could make eye contact with each other, a huge blast erupted right next to Ailin's feet and sent him flying through the air.

The pressure of the explosion tried to knock me off my feet, even through Ailin's shield, but I planted my feet and did my best to ignore it as fear wrapped its way around my heart. I couldn't take my eyes off my Ailin.

I reached out with my magic, trying to catch him, but the blast was too big and too quick. I couldn't make it to him in time.

My viramore landed hard on his side and crashed into the van.

With my heart in my throat, I yelled, "Ailin!" and went running.

But my viramore didn't answer.

He didn't even move.

I was pretty sure he wasn't breathing.

Chapter Sixteen

Ailin

"**A**ilin!"

Everything fucking hurt. Fuck, was I even alive? Was this what death felt like?

"Ailin, wake up!"

Pain made it impossible to comprehend the words being yelled at me.

"Oh my god. Ailin, please wake up. You have to be okay. You have to get up."

That voice. I knew that voice. I... wanted to be near that voice. I... I loved that voice.

"Ailin! Wake the fuck up!"

Sebastian? Was that... my... my viramore?

Another surge of agony shot through my body, traveling from my ribs down to my toes and up to my head. What the fuck was wrong with my body?

"A, please. Please, sweetheart."

Seb? Seb, I'm here.

"Ailin."

I felt something wet touch my cheek over and over again, and it took me a long time to realize it was Sera's tongue. She was lying on my chest, licking my face. She must've used our bond to pull herself to me when I was knocked out.

"Ailin, you—no! Get the fuck away from him, you fucking bastard!" I heard a grunt and felt a surge of magic swell around me. "Don't even think about it. You can't have them either!"

I groaned as Seb's words started to make more sense. *Shit.* He was fighting off whoever had attacked me, wasn't he? *Shit, shit, shit.*

I needed to get up. I couldn't even open my eyes, but I needed to—

"Drink this, sweetheart." He held a vial to my lips, and even though I couldn't see anything, I trusted him enough to drink it down. I recognized the taste—a healing tonic. Well, that was a good idea if I ever heard one.

As quickly as I could, I swallowed it down, then I reached my hand down to feel for the grass. Obviously, I couldn't make a healing bed for myself when we were in the middle of a fight, but I could draw energy from the earth itself to help give myself a boost.

Hopefully enough energy to help me shake this off, get the fuck up, and stop whoever was attacking us.

"Ailin?"

I hummed.

"Ailin, I need you to open your eyes. Please—shit. Hold on, Jorah!"

Jorah? What's wrong with Jorah?

Seb moved away from me, and I felt my heart leap into my throat with sudden and all-consuming fear. His magic swelled, and I could tell he was casting some kind of blast spell. Which meant he was fighting.

Without me.

And our kids were in trouble.

Fuck.

I forced my eyes open. A blue haze surrounded me—a shield—and I could see a van right beside me that was also under the shield. Right. That was what I'd hit when I went flying, wasn't it? I must've been too close to it to get a shield around only me.

There was a blast large enough to shake the ground, and I heard Jorah and Basil yelling something, making my heart race further. I gently pushed Sera off my chest, and she stood beside me, watching me like a hawk. Using every ounce of adrenaline in my body, I forced myself to sit up and take in the scene.

Seb was standing in front of me, partially blocking my view. He was under the shield with me, guarding me while he threw blasting magic at a target on the other side of the parking lot. I couldn't really tell what the hell he was fighting, but it must've been powerful because Jorah, Thayer, and Basil were also blasting it from different sides, and the enemy still wasn't going down.

And all around us, there were Christmas decorations and toys going wild with teeth and claws. A bunch were latched onto our shield, trying to chew their way through to us, not that they could possibly get through Seb's shield. We were safe from them, but they were still gross to look at.

I could only assume the perp had let a ton of them loose, maybe as a distraction? Or to gain more power when they pulled fear and life essence from us.

On the ground, there were several cursed objects already in pieces or burnt to a crisp. When I saw movement to the side of us, I realized why there were so many burnt to a crisp. Zammerra, who must've pulled herself to Seb at the same time as Sera, blew fire on an attacking toy soldier. Then she started stomping it to the ground, efficiently killing it and putting out the fire.

Luckily, being a dragon meant the magic flying all over the place would simply bounce off her scales and her hide was so thick it was unlikely that the cursed objects could hurt her, so she wasn't in any real danger. But there were a lot of cursed items trying to attack. She would be here all day if she tried taking care of them by herself.

I scanned the yard again and tried to focus on the perp, but I still couldn't see him. I could only tell the guy was flinging black-colored magic all over the place.

Fuck. My viramore and kids were under attack.

I needed to get off my ass and help.

"No, you don't," Seb said. "Stay there, A. We've got this."

And maybe they did, but I couldn't just sit here and watch. I had to help. I had to keep my family safe.

I used the van to help myself up to my feet. Since I still needed the energy from the earth, I transferred the pull from my hands to my feet. I was connected enough to my nature magic that it didn't matter that I had boots on. The magic—the energy—could still easily reach me.

When I stood, I had to close my eyes from the dizzy spell that overtook me, and I leaned back against the van and squinted as I took a few deep breaths.

The elves were still in a shield, but all of them were huddled together in the corner, looking absolutely terrified. *Shit.* Those poor little guys.

A few feet from them, the incubus I'd captured was just standing there with his arms crossed over his chest, watching the fight and not looking the least bit scared. He was in a shield, sure, but it being a stranger's magic, most people would've been scared that the shield wouldn't hold. Not him, apparently. He looked... intrigued, maybe? Interested in the fight, for sure, but beyond that, I didn't know.

And that wasn't what I should've been focusing on anyway.

In my head—no, not my head. In my BCA ear mic, Basil said, "Guys, he's eating my magic again."

That sentence made absolutely no sense to me whatsoever.

Jorah's voice said, "I don't know. Fuck. How is he absorbing so much?"

"Seb," I said. "Move back here."

"No. Stay down, Ailin. We'll handle it."

"Sounds like you're handling it real well." I winced as soon as I said it. Wow, I was an asshole.

"Fuck you." There was no heat in his words, only frustration.

"Sorry."

He waved me off, and I leaned to the side to get a better look at our perp, and my brow furrowed in confusion. The guy, if it even was a guy since I could barely see him, was shrouded in a haze of black shadows. He had a shield around him that was almost too dark to see through, but inside that shield was a storm of dark magic. It was similar to how Basil looked when he used his shadow magic, only this guy's magic was darker and more... oily? Where Basil's magic looked natural and inviting, this guy's was the total opposite.

It looked unnatural, not inviting in the least, and it just sort of exuded evilness.

Great. Sounded like a fun guy.

I gathered up my magic quickly and shot it straight at the guy, then watched in disgust as he sucked it up. His magic sort of absorbed it, and I was horrified when I saw my green magic turn black and oily as it was added to the mix in the perp's shield.

"What the fuck?"

Seb huffed and stepped back to stand beside me so I could see better, saying, "He keeps absorbing our magics, but he can't do everyone's at the same time. We're trying to hit him all at once so some hits actually make it."

As if to prove a point, I watched Seb, Thayer, Jorah, and Basil all throw a spell at him, then wrinkled my nose when two out of the four were absorbed, and the two that hit didn't look like they did a lick of damage to the guy's shield. *Shit.* Just how strong was this guy?

"What is he?"

"I don't know." They all threw another round of spells at him, and again, half were eaten, half hit. But no damage was done.

The guy shot out four blasts of oily magic, and when the orb aimed for Seb and me hit his shield, my eyebrows rose. The guy's magic didn't hurt Seb's shield at all, but it did leave behind an oily residue that slid down the shield, almost like our shield had been hit with dirty water and was now wet.

"Ew."

"Right?" Seb said. "It like... drips for a minute before dissipating."

"It'll go away?"

"Eventually."

"Good. Where's Alec and everyone else?"

"We asked them to stay back. This guy's magic is too strong for some of the others. We don't want anyone else getting hurt."

Huh. That was... not a good sign at all.

They all threw another round with the same result, and the guy threw his disgusting oily orbs at us, making another gross spot on Seb's shield.

Jorah came over the mic, saying, "He's a siphoner! Holy shit, I can't believe I forgot about them."

This time, when they all threw magic, I joined in. The guy—the siphoner—absorbed two and let three of the spells hit his shield. But that felt and looked like a shield that was just as strong as any of ours.

Which meant... we'd be here for a long-ass time before we saw any difference in it. And... and if he was absorbing our magics, didn't that mean he was just getting stronger every time we shot magic at him?

"What's a siphoner?" Thayer asked.

"Uh, give me a second to picture the page." Jorah and his photographic memory.

We attacked again, but I had to wonder if we were doing more harm than good at this point.

Jorah spoke into his mic again. "A siphoner is sort of like a witch, only they can't create their own magic." We went another round with the baddie. "They have to absorb others' magic and energy in order to cast spells. So, yeah, he's absorbing our magic and making it his own."

"Then maybe we should stop throwing magic at him?" I asked even as we went yet another round. "Aren't we just making him stronger?"

Thayer hesitated for a beat. "Well, yes. We are. But what else are we supposed to do right now? We can't let him get away, and I think if we stop fighting him, he'll just leave, and we won't be able to stop him."

True enough.

Seb asked, "Jor, how do we stop him?"

"The only way to stop a siphoner is to either wait until he runs out of his magic and take him out by mundane ways. Or we siphon his magic ourselves."

"You mean, we need to suck his freaking disgusting magic out?" My viramore had such a way with words.

"Yes."

"Okay, so how the hell do we do that?" Basil asked.

"I... don't know. We need an artifact or something that can do it."

We went another round, and I grimaced when I watched the dickhead absorb Seb's magic. I... did not like the thought of that at all. No one was allowed access to my viramore's magic like that. No one. Ever. Especially not some evil maniac dickhead.

Sera let out a growl at my feet. She was now in her black leopard form and allowing me to lean a little of my body weight on her, which I gratefully appreciated.

Seb reached over without looking at me and gave my arm a squeeze as he asked Jorah, "Do you know of any? Like, can we send the others out to get something we can use?"

Even from here, I could see Jorah's frustration. "I don't know."

"Fuck," Seb said to only me. "What the hell are we going to do, A?"

I mentally ran through every artifact and magical item we had in our basement, but I honestly couldn't think of a single one that would help us. But then my eyes went over to Seb and the very big staff he was holding in his hands.

"We're so stupid."

"Huh?"

"Your staff. You can use your staff, can't you?"

Seb sort of blinked and glanced around for a second before staring at his staff. Then he turned to me. "Holy shit. Yes. My staff can definitely do it, but... I need to be a lot closer than this."

I nodded. "That's doable." Then, over the mic, I said to the kids, "Seb's staff can absorb the magic, but we need to move closer."

Bas said, "We'll watch your backs, and once you're close enough, we can create a distraction so he doesn't notice right away."

"Sounds like a plan to me."

Seb said to only me, "You can wait here. I'll go up alone so you don't have to walk."

"I can walk—"

"No. You can stay the fuck here, Ailin Ellwood."

"Sorry, baby, but I'm coming. Between the healing tonic and the nature magic I've been using, I'm fine." Was I a hundred percent? Not even close. But I'd have to be dead to let my viramore move closer to some powerful being we knew so little about that was trying to kill us.

"Fine. But don't get hurt again or I'll kick your ass myself."

That made me smile. "Deal."

He rolled his eyes, then started moving closer to the siphoner, and I was right there beside him for every step, albeit a bit shakier. Luckily, Sera walked with me, helping me immensely. I wasn't great, but I was going to do this with my viramore anyway. No way would I wait all the way by the van when this siphoner was so dangerous.

We had to dodge a ton of toys and decor that were still trying to attack us.

We moved as close as we could before the guy tried backing up. Luckily, Bas, Thay, and Jor had surrounded the bastard while I was down and out, so he had nowhere to go.

In my head, Seb said, *"It's not working. His shield is too powerful. I need... I need to touch his shield with my staff. That's the only way it'll work."*

Which meant he was going to have to drop his own shield in order to reach it. *"Like hell you're dropping your shield."*

"It's the only way, Ailin."

"No."

"Sweetheart, I know you're hurting and stressed, so I'm trying to give you the benefit of the doubt, but you're not bossing me around either, okay, asshat? I'm doing this because I'm the only one who can. You're just gonna have to deal."

Fuck, fuck, fuckity, fuck. He was... he was right. But I didn't want to put him in danger. He needed to stay under a shield.

Seb sighed in my head. *"A, it'll be fine. You guys keep him distracted, and I'll get started. Watch my back."*

Fuck. Fuck! *"You promise me you'll be okay?"*

"Yes. I promise."

Fucking hell. *"Fine. But I'm not happy about this plan. At all."*

"Noted. Now, make yourself a shield."

I did as he asked, pulling a shield over the top of Sera and me under Seb's shield. My viramore shrunk his own shield down to cover only himself, fully separating us. I really fucking hated this plan. So fucking much.

I took a deep breath. *"I'll move farther to the right and attack to distract him, and you can do your thing."*

"Thank you, sweetheart."

"Don't sweetheart me. I'm mad at you."

He sighed in my head again but didn't say anything else, so I moved forward with our plan.

I stepped to the side with Sera against my legs and started blasting the siphoner with magic. Spell after spell after spell. I hit him with small blasts, big ones, with wind, with pure power. And then I reached out with my nature magic, found a bunch of branches that must've fallen off the trees behind the building, and made them fly.

I knew they wouldn't do any harm to the guy's shield or anything, but they would—hopefully—serve as a good distraction.

The guy hit the branches with magic, making them blast apart in the air, and that just pissed me off. Maybe those branches were dead already, but that didn't give him the right to destroy a part of nature. Fucking asshole.

Out of the corner of my eye, I saw Seb drop his shield, press his staff right up against the siphoner's shield, and the orb on the end of the staff glowed yellow. I kept flinging magic, sticks, leaves, and rocks at the guy, trying to keep his attention. I'd rather him eat up all my magic than realize what Seb was doing and start attacking him.

The kids attacked him as well, keeping the guy more than busy with all of us.

I pulled on my magic, creating a huge glowing orb of power, hoping it would be too appetizing for the guy to ignore, and threw it at him. As predicted, he pulled the magic into himself and his shield, and the green morphed into black as the guy smiled cruelly at me.

But then he froze for only a millisecond, and I knew the jig was up.

He turned, saw what Seb was doing, and threw a big oily black orb at him. I couldn't throw a shield in front of my viramore like I wanted because that would either break the staff's connection to the siphoner's magic, or it simply wouldn't work because there was nowhere for the shield to go.

Instead, I quickly gathered another power orb and threw it at the si-phoner's spell, trying to knock it off course while my heart thumped hard in my chest. I felt like letting out a joyous yell when it worked, and his spell flew past Seb and hit the ground, harming no one.

But of course the siphoner wasn't finished. He lobbed three more spells at Seb, and I heard Bas yell, "I got the left one, Dad!"

Showing a huge amount of trust in my kid, I ignored the one farthest to the left and sent two of my own orbs at the other two.

All three attacks were taken down, and I yelled in my head to Seb, *"Hurry the fuck up, baby."*

"Almost done. Give me a few more seconds."

Bas and I knocked down four more attacks before Seb yelled out loud, "Got it!"

As soon as the words were out of his mouth, the siphoner's shield fell. He was still surrounded by a cloud of magic, but it was a hell of a lot better than it'd been a minute ago.

Only a second later, all three of my kids had their tranq guns raised. They all fired, and the siphoner used his magic to hit the darts out of the way and to the ground, blocking each hit.

As the siphoner fought back, flinging magic everywhere, I focused on defense, making sure my kids and Seb were safe.

Because he was distracted with physical blows, he didn't see my viramore move closer to him. Seb used the staff's length to stretch across the space and into the cloud of magic circling the man.

Seb's staff glowed yellow for a moment before it mixed with his blue enchanter magic. And then, a few seconds later, it started to darken as it sucked up the ambient magic around the siphoner.

The siphoner started to panic when he realized his magic was being taken away. He screamed as if he was in horrible pain—for all I knew, it really did hurt him, but I didn't think so. In his panic, he missed one of the kids' darts, but he was so worked up that it didn't take him down. At least not right away.

The guy fell to his knees, though, still screaming and crying, and I watched in mild horror as my viramore stepped even closer to him, still pulling on the guy's magic, pulling on his soul. Souls were linked to magic, and now that the siphoner had no magic left, it looked like Seb's staff was going for the very essence of the man.

"Seb, you can back off now," I said, surprised he was still going when the guy was down and out of magic. When Seb didn't respond, I stepped closer. "Seb. Stop."

He still didn't stop.

I moved up next to him and placed my hand on his staff-arm, gently tugging it away from the siphoner. "Seb? Baby, you need to stop." I gave his arm a little shake. "Sebastian! Stop!"

Finally, he snapped out of whatever trance he was in, blinked, and a horror-filled expression crossed his face a moment before he cut the staff off and stepped back.

"Ailin..." He sounded horrified.

"It's okay, baby. You're okay, and so is he." I glanced down at the siphoner, who was passed out—from the tranq, not from Seb's staff. Thayer was cuffing the man with special handcuffs made for supernaturals. "You did good, baby." I put my hand on the small of Seb's back and leaned in to kiss his cheek since I could feel how upset he was.

"The staff... it... it wanted to consume him. Once it felt all that power, it just... it didn't want to let go. It hasn't taken over like that since I first started using it." That was probably fifty years ago, so I could understand why he was freaked out.

"It's okay."

"I could've killed him."

I wanted to say *so what? He deserves it.* But I knew that wasn't the right response. "But you didn't."

"I could have."

I sucked in a breath. "Baby, everything's okay. That dickhead's fine, and no one's hurt—"

"You're still hurt, Ailin."

I huffed. "I'm fine."

He sent me a small glare, but I was glad he was focused on that rather than the siphoner or the staff.

"Come on, let's help Zamm kill the rest of these damned cursed objects, get the elves back home, and take in the prisoners."

That made Seb glance at the incubus, who was still standing there with his arms crossed over his chest. "Where did that guy come from? Why's he here?"

"I don't know, but I'm sure we'll find out." I kissed his cheek again. "Ready?"

"As ready as I'll ever be, I guess."

With one more squeeze of comfort, I released him, turned around, and jumped back into the fray.

Chapter Seventeen

Seb

It was late as hell by the time I finished helping with the leftover cursed objects, and Ailin got the elves settled at home—I was pretty sure they were there to stay. Afterward, we met back at HQ where they'd taken the siphoner and incubus and got to work on IDing the perps and finding out absolutely everything we could about them.

God, did I feel like such an asshole for letting my staff overtake me like that. I'd left the staff at home, in the basement, where it was going to stay for a little while because that had been... terrifying.

I needed to evaluate my connection with the thing and make sure that never, ever, ever happened again. If I couldn't control it, I was going to put the damn thing in our basement under lock and key for the rest of time.

But... hopefully, I'd be able to figure out what the fuck happened because that staff had saved our asses on more than one occasion.

Over the course of a couple of hours, I had Ailin take two more healing tonics, so he was feeling a lot better by the time we were finished gathering everything we could find on both the incubus and the siphoner.

Since the siphoner was still waking up from the tranq, Ailin and I went to interview the incubus first, taking both folders filled with information on the perps with us. I wasn't sure how Ailin had made Alec agree to let us interview both of them, but I wasn't about to complain. I wanted to know what the hell was going on here.

As soon as we sat down, Ailin asked the guy, "Why were you at the factory tonight?"

The guy stared at Ailin, saying nothing.

"Were you planning on hurting the elves?"

Still nothing.

"Were you going to take them back to the siphoner?"

The man said nothing, but he did sort of twitch, which made me think Ailin was onto something there.

My viramore glared at the man. "I'd ask you your name, but we already know everything since you had your ID on you. I was honestly surprised it was your real ID. You have a record, Emros Vakal. Mostly petty theft and trespassing. It looks like you've been living a little rough the past ten years, but your arrest rate went up significantly five years ago. What exactly happened to you to make you take such risks? Usually you're arrested with a succubus named Olrithe Ennelis. We have people bringing her in now."

The incubus—Emros—jerked in his seat and glared hard at Ailin. "Why would you do that? She has nothing to do with this. She wasn't even there."

"Finally, a reaction," Ailin said privately to me.

Ailin shrugged like he didn't have a care in the world. "Maybe, but it seemed like it was worth pursuing. I'm sure we can find a reason to hold her for a while."

True anger crossed Emros's features. "Leave her alone. Olrithe had nothing to do with any of this."

"We'll see about that."

The man growled and banged on the table. "Leave her alone! She had nothing to do with this fucking plan Mor—" He grunted in pain and bent over, raising his cuffed hands to his throat as he groaned.

I asked Ailin, *"This fucking plan Mortimer came up with?"*

"That's exactly what I think he was gonna say." Ailin nodded and spoke out loud to Emros. "That's what I thought. He has you under a compulsion too, doesn't he?"

Emros sent Ailin another glare and managed a minute nod before groaning in pain again.

"Well, fuck." Ailin sighed, long and loud. "We're not going to get anything out of him as long as he's under the compulsion." In my head, he added, *"We'll have to question him again once we break it."*

"You really think you can break the binds?"

"Yes. I've done it before, and I'll figure it out once we talk to fucking Mortimer."

"Sounds like a plan."

Ailin and I stood as he spoke. "Someone will take you to a holding cell."

"Wait. That's it? Can't I go home?"

"Not yet."

"But I didn't do anything."

My viramore leaned down to meet the guy's gaze. "We want to keep you here until we sort everything out with the siphoner, okay? We want to help."

The incubus blinked in surprise before sitting up straight. "You want to help... me?" He sounded so surprised, as if no one in his whole life had ever helped him.

From the look of his profile, I was afraid that might be true. It made me feel for the guy. He truly hadn't done anything wrong at the factory, and I was sure he hadn't been there by choice. We were going to figure out a way to help him, and the elves too.

"Yes. We don't *want* to help. We're *going to* help."

"Really?"

"Really."

"Oh-okay."

I gave the dazed guy a nod, and the two of us headed out of the room. Ailin didn't hesitate to walk to the next interrogation room, so I followed him inside. He didn't even check in with Alec, despite the poor werewolf coming out of the observation room and heading in our direction.

"You really are an asshole sometimes," I muttered under my breath.

Ailin shot me a wink. "I know." He sat at the table across from the siphoner, and said, "So... Mr. Mortimer Tombend, is it?"

The man in question smirked at my viramore but didn't say anything, and I eyed the man. He looked so... normal now that his magic wasn't swirling around him in a storm of destruction. The guy had short brown hair, brown eyes, light skin, some scruff on his cheeks, and was probably around five-ten-ish, if I had to guess. He was skinny as all hell, to the point that he almost looked unhealthy.

All in all, if I walked past him on the street, I never would've guessed he was some evil asshole, let alone a rare creature I'd never really heard about before now.

That was probably how he was able to steal someone's powers. He looked so innocent and non-threatening that I was sure people let their guard down around him. Then he could strike without the other person ever realizing he was a threat.

What a dick.

"What was the plan here, Mortimer? You decided to attack the city and gain all that power? For what purpose? What did you intend to do? Take over? Run the city?"

The man just shrugged, but he still looked smug.

Ailin shuffled some papers around in the folder he was carrying, putting on a little show for the dickhead. "Or... maybe you wanted to break into the prison and get your baby brother out? I hear he's serving two life sentences for murder, breaking and entering, and assault. Maybe he can share his cell with you."

The man's smirk fell, and he glared daggers at Ailin.

"Ohhhh, so that was it, huh? You wanted to break your brother out of prison, but you don't have enough power on your own. You needed to steal a shit-ton of power from others, and to do so, you terrorized the entire city for a week."

"You have no proof it was me. Those elves are the ones who cursed everything."

"True, true." Ailin leaned in close. "But I can feel the bind you put on them and the incubus, and you know what, Mortimer?"

Mortimer made a little growling sound.

"My word holds a lot more clout than yours, and I'm not the only witch in this building who can feel it. We have more eyewitnesses to your bindings than you can count."

The man let out a small laugh and waved him off. "Yeah, sure. If you say so."

Ailin ignored him. "You know what else, Mortimer?"

The man met my viramore's gaze, lifted a brow, and shrugged one shoulder.

When Ailin spoke, his voice was quiet but rang with power. "I'm gonna break each and every bind you have."

The man actually laughed at that, like it was the funniest thing he ever heard. "Even if what you say is true, that I have binds on other people—and I'm not claiming I do—you wouldn't be able to break them. No one can break a bind but the person that laid it."

Ailin smirked. "Wanna bet?"

Then my viramore stood, released his magic in a wave of green, and leaned over the table, putting his hand on the siphoner's chest. The man tried to back away, but Ailin's magic was already wrapped around him, holding him tight and not letting him go.

Because of the supernatural handcuffs, the siphoner's innate magic didn't work, so he couldn't siphon Ailin's magic, thank god. He was completely at the mercy of my viramore.

A small part of me enjoyed that, enjoyed the fact that this horrible man had zero control right now.

I watched Ailin's green magic slide inside Mortimer's mouth, nose, and ears, and I had no doubt that it was seeking out the siphoner's heart and soul.

"Let go of me," he growled out, wiggling around, still trying to break free.

Ailin didn't say anything. He simply closed his eyes and concentrated while I watched on. There wasn't really anything I could do to help him unless he needed an extra boost of magic.

Through our link, I asked, *"Do you need my help to break it?"*

"Maybe. I might be able to do it myself, but I wouldn't mind your help."

Since I was sitting beside him, I reached over and placed my hand on Ailin's back, then I released my magic and asked it to find Ailin's. It didn't really need the direction because it always sought his magic out, no matter what we were doing.

My blue magic mixed with his green, and I watched it float its way into the siphoner's mouth, nose, and ears. Then I closed my eyes and let myself feel.

Ailin led the way, and I let him. He wrapped our magics around the man's heart before it permeated through it. It didn't take long to feel the very core of Mortimer, and I kinda wished I hadn't felt it because it was sort of oily, like his magic had been.

But even with the oiliness, his soul was a soft glow inside his chest. A dark one, sure, but there was still a glow there.

Our magics wrapped around it and through it, and after a few seconds, I sensed something that felt like a string that was tied to his soul. I let my magic tug on it, and when it vibrated, I could feel the essence of the elves on the other side. It was strange because this end of the string was one solid string wrapped around his heart, but when I followed the strand, I could tell it broke off into multiple ones, flowing into each and every elf on our coven land.

I could only guess that Mortimer had conned his way into binding the whole troupe as a group instead of doing each individual separately.

"Nice work, baby," Ailin said as he used our magics to form almost a large knife. Then he lifted it and chopped it through the string.

I felt the snap reverberate through the siphoner's entire body, and I heard the man scream out in shock and pain.

Then he started cussing up a storm and thrashing around even more than before. He sounded like a rabid animal. But we ignored him and went searching for the other binds.

It didn't take long for Ailin to find the string attached to the incubus, and after a few seconds, we cut that one as well, setting Emros free.

The siphoner was even more pissed off now.

But that didn't stop us from searching for any other binds in his soul.

We needed to make sure this evil man couldn't control anyone ever again.

We found two more—one that felt like it was attached to a satyr, and one to a succubus who was likely Emros's friend. We snapped those two as well, freeing everyone from the siphoner's hold.

It felt good, knowing we'd freed so many people from a life of misery under this evil siphoner's rule.

When we pulled away, Mortimer was a sweaty, horrible mess. He looked pale, exhausted, and pissed off beyond belief.

He looked ready to attack us, but snapping those bindings had worn the man out—not that he could hurt us when wearing cuffs and magicless anyway.

"Now that that's done, you wanna tell us more about your brother?"

The man let out a loud growl before jumping up and diving across the table, aiming for Ailin's throat. I threw up a shield without thinking and used a small power orb to push the bastard back into his seat.

When he landed on his ass, he looked surprised and dazed, and I turned to my viramore, saying, "Can we go home now? We know why he did it. Let's let someone else take over the interrogations. I want to be done with this miserable dickhead."

Ailin blew out a breath. "Fine." In my head, he said, *"Let's check on Emros first, just to make sure he's alright before we leave the premises."*

"Sounds good."

As we headed for the door, the siphoner yelled, "I'll kill you for this! This isn't over, Ailin and Sebastian Ellwood! You better watch your backs because I'm coming after yo—"

Ailin slammed the door before the horrible man could continue his rant. Neither one of us was worried about the dickhead coming after us because he wouldn't be seeing the light of day for a very, very long time.

We headed back to the holding cells, and when we reached Emros's cell, I was a little surprised to find him crying.

Oh god, did we hurt him when we cut the bindings?

Shit. Were the elves hurting too?

I didn't think it'd hurt them. Shit, shit, shit. That was the last thing I wanted to do.

The incubus looked up at us, met Ailin's eyes, and smiled through his tears. "You... you freed me."

Ailin gave him a slight smile. "Are you alright?"

Emros nodded. "I... you... thank you. Mother of All, thank you."

"You're welcome."

Emros stood and moved closer to the edge of his cell. "I'll tell you everything you want. Everything. Mortimer tricked me. We met at a bar, and I went home with him. I thought we were gonna have a fun night together, but when he got me on his bed, I realized he'd trapped me in a witch's circle. I couldn't get out, and he bound me to him against my will."

"I'm sorry you had to go through that," I said, an ache in my heart for everything he went through.

Emros nodded. "Thanks. Um... he did pretty much the same thing to Olrithe about three years ago, I think. It's like he's been collecting... slaves for years." He shook his head, looking upset. "He's made me do so much horrible shit. Oh, and he's trying to break his brother out of prison—that's why he's doing all this crazy shit."

"Thank you, Emros," Ailin said, cutting him off. "Would it be okay if you came back to the interrogation room so we can record everything?"

"Of course."

We ended up speaking to Emros for a few hours, detailing everything the poor man had been forced to do for the last five years. Everything we'd discovered and pieced together about Mortimer's motives were confirmed by the incubus. Breaking his brother out of prison had been his main motive. It sounded like Mortimer had lost his mind a little along the way, and we ended up with all this horrible shit happening to the citizens of our city.

By the time we were leaving HQ, the sun was up, and I was dead on my feet. Ailin was even worse than me because he'd been so injured earlier. He needed sleep. Badly. We both did.

So once we finished the interview, I told Alec we were going home and would come back later for any paperwork or anything else he needed. Then I grabbed Ailin's hand and dragged him out of there.

When we parked the car at home, Ailin was half asleep, so I walked around to the passenger's side, pulled him to his feet, and wrapped an arm around him to help him into the house.

I'd already sent a text in the family chat, letting everyone know we needed to sleep today and to wait until dinnertime to contact us or come to the big house. They all agreed, and I figured half the usual culprits—Bas, Thay, Jor, and Clover—would be sleeping the day away too since they were on the case with us, so hopefully, we'd have a good bit of rest today.

After all of that, I was surprised to hear voices when I pushed the front door open. I sighed and tugged Ailin along toward the living room but paused when I realized I didn't recognize any of the voices and that they were speaking Fae'lee.

Had... had someone broken into our house? But how? No one could've gotten through our wards.

I heard another voice that sounded mildly familiar.

"What the fuck?"

Ailin stiffened for only a second before blowing out a breath. "It's the elves."

I froze. "What? You let the elves inside the house?"

Ailin shrugged a little. "Only the first floor. Just..." He waved me on. "Go look."

I pulled him with me the rest of the way, then froze at the sight before me.

There was Winter Solstice wrapping paper, ribbons, tape, and bows all over the living and dining rooms. And elves were... *everywhere*. On the couches, rolling around on the floor, on the dining table, literally climbing the wall, hanging from the ceiling, and jumping from a bookshelf to land on the couch. Just... just everywhere.

"Ailin, what have you done?"

He sighed. "Baby, look." He motioned to the corner of the room, and I blinked.

There was a pile of presents, all wrapped up neat and beautiful and perfect.

"Are those...?"

"Yep. Our gifts. When I brought them back from the factory, I asked the elves if they wanted to go back to Faela. But they like it here, surprisingly after everything they've been through. They asked to stay here with us—I think they're taking over the shed officially—and they wanted to repay us for our hospitality and help capturing Mortimer. Nimeroni overheard us talking about needing to wrap presents, and she offered. I checked that you had stickers with names on each gift, and you did, so it was easy to hand it over to them."

I glanced around and took a better look, realizing that some of the elves on the floor were actually in the process of wrapping more of the presents. I mean, they looked like they were also playing by rolling the wrapping paper around themselves and dancing around with ribbon, but if I looked closely, I could see them wrapping a gift at the same time.

I glanced at the gifts in the corner again.

They seriously looked beautiful. Almost too pretty to rip open and way better than anything I'd ever wrapped in my life. Wow.

It looked like absolute chaos, but apparently, they still knew how to get shit done.

"Holy shit." I sagged in something like relief. "We have time to actually prepare the food and everything else." I'd been getting overwhelmed with the amount of shit we needed to do before Winter Solstice, so this was an immense help.

"Yep." He squeezed my waist. "Now, let's go to bed."

I gave him a nod, but before we walked away, I loudly said in Fae'lee, "Thank you all so much for your help."

Nimeroni looked up from where she was taping some wrapping paper and sent me a wide smile. "It's our pleasure."

A bunch of the others said similar things, all of the elves smiling at us as they continued to play.

She rushed over and wrapped her little body around Ailin's leg, then around mine, giving us hugs.

I patted her back.

"Thank you for freeing us. We... we're so very grateful."

That made me smile, and Ailin offered her one too. "No problem. I'm glad you're free, and I'm happy to have you here on our land."

She let out a small squeal of excitement, then gave our legs each another hug before rushing back over to help with the wrapping.

Ailin said, "We're going upstairs to sleep for a long time. Help yourselves to the kitchen."

"Do you really think that's a good idea? It's going to be a disaster."

"I know, but I'd rather them do that than try to wake us up because they're starving."

I hummed. *"Or, god, have them find Bramble and ask him for food."*

That made Ailin snort, and I sent him a smile before leading him up to our bedroom where we could fall into our bed for a very, very long time... hopefully.

Chapter Eighteen

Seb

Winter Solstice was finally here and already in full swing despite the fact that we were still waiting for half the family to show up. Ailin and I had woken up super early to get food in the oven and on the stove, but luckily, a bunch of the kids had come over yesterday to help set up the backyard with lots of tables, chairs, and decorations.

It looked great out there. There were fairy lights hanging across the top of the yard and in the trees surrounding it, making pretty, warm lighting. Strands of paper snowflakes hung throughout the yard with specks of blue glitter and streamers strewn about, plus decorative pinecones and fake snow in very specific spots—our daughter, Leilani, was very particular in her decorating, and it honestly paid off. It'd turned out really beautiful.

We had tables full of food, even after all the early birds had done a round. We'd continue refilling the food throughout the day so everyone could eat to their heart's content. We'd made enough food to feed an army, so I was sure we'd even have leftovers. Or at least I hoped so.

Not everyone was here yet since it was still kinda early. We were waiting for our Gauhala crew and a couple of families that'd had to go to the in-laws' celebration first, so we hadn't opened presents yet. Much to the dismay of all the little kids that were already here.

There was a humongous pile of presents on, under, and in front of the present table, so I knew the kids were dying. Once everyone got here, we'd let them dig in and hand everything out.

Even the elves were running around, playing games with all the kids, and it looked like everyone was having a great time. So hopefully that meant having the elves here would work out in the long term.

They'd already taken over the shed and made it their own, so Ailin had to ask another tree to form a smaller shed for us to store our outdoor tables, chairs, movie projector, and screen for our big family movie nights. But that was no big deal. The trees on our land were always more than happy to accommodate my viramore.

I still hadn't gone down to the basement to check out my staff, and I honestly wasn't sure I wanted to anytime soon. I knew avoiding it was probably only building the problem up in my head more, but I just wasn't ready yet.

I was sure Ailin would help me soon enough, though, so I wasn't too worried about it.

When I checked the time, I found myself migrating over to the small shed we'd built for the Gauhala portal. Delaro had created a new type of portal, and he set one end up in our front yard and the other end in Remi's yard in Gauhala. We'd all decided to make sure the portals were heavily guarded, so Ailin had asked a few trees to build a shed around it, and we added extra wards so only family could exit the shed itself. Just in case one end of the portal ended up in the wrong hands. I didn't see that happening because they were so well-warded, but Ailin was nothing if not overcautious when it came to the safety of our coven.

Remi, Tan, and the rest of the Gauhala crew were due any minute, and I wanted to greet them as soon as they got here. I missed having Remi and Tan here every day, but they were both so damn happy with their viramores in Gauhala that I couldn't be angry about it. And now that we had the portal, it made visits so much easier.

Almost as soon as I reached the portal shed, Remi walked out the door. He smiled when he saw me and walked over to give me a hug, saying, "Hey, Pops."

"Hey, bud. How're you doing?"

"I'm really good." He released me and smiled before turning and grabbing a large bag from his viramore, Bel.

I pulled Bel, Remi's viramore, into a bear hug because I knew the kid needed more familial hugs in his life. "It's so good to see you."

"You too, Seb."

When I released him, I saw Ailin headed our way, and I shot my viramore a grin. We were both always so happy when our entire family was able to get together.

Tan was next in line, and I pulled the kid into a tight hug. He too needed extra familial hugs. "So good to see you."

"Right back 'atcha."

Garrick, Tan's viramore, was behind him, and even though the dragon shifter was a little standoffish at times, I still gave him a quick hug.

Then Oakley came into view, and I couldn't help but smile widely at the kid. They were Garrick's only child, so also a dragon shifter, and they'd had a really rough childhood, thanks to being kidnapped as a baby. Garrick had only recently gotten his kid back into his life, and I was so grateful for it. At twenty-five, Oakley was technically an adult, but anyone younger than my own kids counted as a kid in my eyes.

"Hey, Oakley," I said with a smile. "I'm so happy to have you here. Can I give you a hug?"

They seemed unsure but still nodded.

So I pulled them in and was relieved when they sank into me and hugged me back.

Quietly, I said, "I really am glad you're here. If you need anything today, don't hesitate to ask me, although I'm sure Tan would love to help you."

That got a small snort out of them as they released me. "Thank you, and you're right. Tan will be all over it."

We shared a smile before Ailin came over, saying, "Can I get a hug too, kiddo?"

It took Oakley a second to realize Ailin was talking to them, and when they did, they blushed a little but went in for the hug anyway.

When Ailin released them, he walked over to Garrick, and the two of them did a sort of bro-hug kind of thing that looked incredibly awkward and ridiculous. It wasn't often my viramore was awkward, so I found my eyes drawn to him.

And then Ailin made it worse by saying to Garrick, "Good to see you, kiddo."

They both froze, and I couldn't help the snort that escaped me. Garrick was, like, over fifteen hundred years old. Calling him *kiddo* was the most ridiculous thing I'd ever heard Ailin do.

And he'd done some really ridiculous things over the years.

Ailin shook his head with a grimace. "Yeah, no, that's... that's weird. Sorry. I don't even... yeah, no. Let's forget I ever said that. Please."

"Agreed. You never said... whatever that was." Garrick gave him a nod that Ailin returned, and I caught Tan's eye before we both burst out in laughter. Even Oakley, Remi, and Bel joined in.

While we all cracked up at them, I saw Keryth and his sisters—Bel's cousins—arrive.

As Tan teased Garrick, Bel met his cousins near the shed, and I overheard Ker ask him, "Are you sure it's okay that we're here?"

Without hesitation, Bel said, "Yes, of course."

But that wasn't good enough for me because Ker still looked unsure.

So I walked over and pulled Keryth into a hug, saying, "You're a part of our family now, Ker. You're a part of our coven, and we want you and your girls here. I promise you we do." God, it killed me that he didn't already know that. To Ailin, through our bond, I said, *"We need to do a better job of making sure Ker knows he and the girls are Ellwoods now."*

The poor kid had been through a lot in his short life, and he wasn't used to relying on anyone but himself. He wasn't used to having a family.

We needed to change that.

"Agreed."

Ker took a deep breath as he hugged me back before nodding and whispering, "Okay... okay. Thank you."

"Anytime." I gave him one last squeeze before finally releasing him.

Then I made sure to give each of Ker's sisters a hug—Alsira, Gemma, Saranor, and Zellya. They were a good group of half-fae kids that I already loved to death and was excited to spoil. I couldn't wait to see if they liked all the presents we'd bought them.

Once everyone was hugged by Ailin and me, I said, "Alright, guys, let's go to the backyard. I know everyone's excited to see you. And the kids are dying to open their presents."

To my surprise and delight, the girls took off running, giggling as they met up with some of our other grandkids. They jumped right into the game they were playing, and I was relieved. Ker and the girls had been coming to our family movie nights for months, so I was happy the girls were comfortable here.

It took forever to get through all the gifts, and I was sort of dying to go get my gift for Ailin. He had no idea what I'd gotten him. For once, I'd done a good job of keeping it from him. I'd even had Emrys and Julius—two vampires in our coven—hold onto his gift last night so he wouldn't see it before today.

"Here, baby," Ailin said, handing me a present before he retook the seat beside me.

I took it with a smile and opened the pretty wrapping paper, feeling a little bad about ripping it when the elves had done such an amazing job.

When I opened the box, my eyebrows rose in surprise. A photo album sat inside, so I gingerly took it out and opened it up. As I flicked through the pages, my eyes felt a little misty.

Every page had pictures of our family and of the two of us that we'd taken over the last few years. It had to have taken Ailin a long-ass time to go through the hundreds of pictures we had on our phones and pick out the best ones. The time and effort of this gift was so meaningful to me.

And I'd had no idea, so it was the best surprise.

"Thank you, A. I... I don't even know how to thank you. This is beautiful." I glanced up at him with a watery smile.

He grinned back and leaned in for a soft kiss. "You're welcome, baby. I'm glad you like it."

"Like it? I fucking love it."

That made him chuckle and pull me in for a hug and another kiss before we drew our attention back to Niya, who was, of course, making a big show about opening her present. My god, that girl loved to be the center of attention. She was a goofball, and I adored her.

A little while later, I smiled down at my gift that I hadn't wanted to put down yet. I still couldn't believe my viramore had given me such a thoughtful gift. This might've been my favorite present I'd ever received.

I leaned over and kissed Ailin's temple. "Thank you, sweetheart."

He eyed me. "That's the tenth time you've thanked me. You don't have to keep saying it. I know you like it." He sent me a small smile. "I'm glad you do."

"I'll treasure it forever."

He rolled his eyes with a grin and leaned over to kiss my lips, then whispered against them, "I know you will. Now stop thanking me. Please."

I laughed, then pulled him in for a hard kiss. I kept it mostly chaste since we were surrounded by people—people who would totally start fake-gagging if I even hinted at tongue—even though I really wanted to deepen it.

"Later."

I hummed in agreement, gave him one last peck, and released him. "Okay, now it's time to get your present."

Ailin clapped his hands together and rubbed them. "I can't wait to see what you've been so secretive about."

He made me chuckle, and I stood, then kissed the top of his head and walked over to Emrys. "Do you mind if we grab Ailin's present now?"

Em sent me a smile. "No problem. I'll go grab it."

And then he was gone, using his vampire speed to run along the pathway to his home on coven land. I'd been planning on going with him, but apparently, he'd decided to leave my slow ass here. But I walked to the edge of the treeline to wait.

Emrys was a good friend—a good family member—and sometimes I thought back to when I first met him and had absolutely hated the guy. He'd been a bit of an ass, truth be told, but he'd had a good reason to be, and I'd been... super jealous of his relationship with Ailin. Regardless, I was happy he was a part of our family now.

I glanced back at Ailin because I knew he was watching me, curious about what I had up my sleeve. I was nervous-excited about it. I knew he'd love it, but... I wasn't sure *I* would.

Oh my god, I was probably making a horrible, terrible mistake with this. It was so much responsibility, but... but it would make my Ailin happy, so I guess I was willing to sacrifice for it.

Emrys reappeared only a few minutes later. So with a deep breath, I retrieved the wiggling box from him.

"Thank you so much for keeping them last night for me," I said with a bright smile aimed at the vampire. I'd picked up the gift yesterday, and Emrys and Julius had hidden it for me in their house. Since they'd come back home from their special assignment a few cities over, their house had seemed like the best hiding place.

He grinned back. "No problem. I can't wait to see his face."

"Me either."

He patted my back, and the two of us headed back over to Ailin while I second-guessed my decision the whole way.

Chapter Nineteen

Ailin

I could tell Seb was up to something and that he was nervous about it, but I pretended not to notice since I knew it had something to do with my gift. I had absolutely no idea what in the world was making him feel that way, but I was excited to see it.

Whatever it was, I had no doubt it'd be interesting and likely something I'd love since my viramore was really good at gift giving.

So when he came back into the yard with Emrys in tow, carrying a gigantic box wrapped in Solstice paper, I didn't hesitate to jump up and head his way.

Seb could barely see over the top of the box, but when he caught a glimpse of me, he said, "Wait! Go sit down. I'm bringing it to you."

"But—"

"No, A, go sit. Please."

I sighed but complied since I didn't want to mess with his whole plan. He'd never forgive me if I messed up the surprise after all his sneaking around.

When he came over and started to pass me the box, I hesitated and asked, "It's not a doll, is it?"

A burst of laughter came out of him, and I glared, but then I noticed the box wiggle... as if reacting to the sound.

My eyes widened. "Holy shit, it *is* a doll."

He kept laughing. "No, it's not. I promise."

I could feel the truth in his statement, but if it wasn't a cursed doll and the box was wiggling...

My eyes widened. Holy shit. He didn't, did he? He couldn't have... Mother of All, did he get me a...

I quickly took the box from him. Only when I had it in my lap did I realize the top of the box was completely open. I peeked inside and about died on the spot.

There were two... black and brown puppies inside.

Puppies!

Holy fucking shit. My viramore got me not one but *two* puppies to baby to my heart's content?

Never in my life would I have guessed he'd gotten me *animals*.

"Mother of All!" I let out a sound that was definitely not a scream of delight. "Puppies? You got me puppies?"

"Hellhound puppies, to be exact." He sent me a cautious smile.

My eyes widened further. "Hellhound puppies? But... they... they could be with us for a really long time... like hundreds of years, or maybe forever."

"I know. That's why I got them. I knew you'd fall in love with them, and I didn't want you worrying that they'd... you know, not be here in a decade or two."

"Really?"

He nodded. "Really."

"But... they're gonna get huge."

"Oh, I know."

I looked up at my viramore with a huge smile on my face. "You got me hellhound puppies! Where did you even find them?"

"I went to the supe shelter. They had a bunch of different creatures, but I thought you'd like these two the best since they like to cuddle."

"I love them. I love you." I reached into the box and picked one up—a girl, from the look of it. "Hi there, cutie pie. Oh my Mother, you are so damn adorable." I gave her a kiss and hugged her to my chest, and the little cutie licked my chin. I saw some of her flames erupt around her body, and I was relieved when they didn't burn me.

Hellhounds had hellfire, but most were able to control whether or not it actually harmed someone. It was almost like they had to actively think about harming someone with them. They also didn't always have flames, usually only sprouting them when they were fighting once they were old enough to control them. Being a baby, she wouldn't have control quite yet.

Since I wanted to give the other one the same treatment, I glanced around to find someone else to hold her. My gaze landed on Ker, who sat beside me, so I passed her over to him.

"Uh... I don't know what I'm doing with a puppy."

I smiled at him. "You're used to kids. Puppies can't be harder than that."

He looked unsure but still hugged the cutie to his chest.

So I turned to the other hellhound and picked him up. I double-checked, and yep, he was a boy. "Hi, baby boy." He immediately started licking my chin. "Oh my Mother, you are too sweet and cute." I gave him a kiss and a hug, and before I could do anything else, all the kids were coming over to give the new puppies pets.

Seb said, "I already warded the yard so they can't run into the trees. You can put them down if you want."

I sent him a smile, surprised I hadn't noticed the extra wards on the yard, but then again, we had a million people here today, so I was a bit distracted.

I kissed the puppy, and before I set him down on the ground, I said to the kids, "Give him a little space, okay? Let the puppies come to you. Don't chase them, or you'll scare them."

I got a chorus of *okays* back, and Ker and I set the puppies loose and watched them tumble around with a horde of children laughing and calling them and wanting to play. I watched for a long time, making sure the puppies didn't seem too overwhelmed or stressed from all of the people, but they both seemed like they were having the time of their lives.

"What are you gonna name them?" Seb asked me a little while later. He reached over and laced his fingers with mine, offering a smile that I returned.

"Fifi and Foo-Foo."

He paused and stared at me. "You can't be serious."

"I am."

"Ailin, I'm not standing outside, yelling *Foo-Foo come inside.* No. Just no."

I chuckled at that. "You don't mind Fifi, though?"

He sighed. "I... guess not."

"Fine... Fifi and Fuzzlet."

He was silent for a beat. "Fuzzlet?"

"Yep. It's the perfect name. Look at how fuzzy his little butt is."

He stared at the puppy that did a little somersault as he dove for a rope toy someone had thrown. "Fuzzlet."

I held in a laugh. "Yes. Fuzzlet."

"Are you... are you sure?"

"Positive. Doesn't he look like a Fuzzlet?"

Seb snorted. "Uh, sure. They're your dogs, so... Fifi and Fuzzlet it is."

He must've been in a really good mood not to argue with me over their ridiculous names. I'd thought for sure he'd put up a fight, and I'd end up having to name them something normal like Spot and Freckles or something. I absolutely didn't think he'd just... let me get away with Fifi and Fuzzlet.

I stared at him, squinting my eyes, wondering if he was doing this on purpose to try and get me to admit I was being ridiculous. But... the man just sat there, not even hinting at joking.

Well, joke's on him because I sure as shit wasn't backing down.

Fifi and Fuzzlet it was then.

I paused and stared at the puppies.

Okay, maybe the joke was on me... because, well, Fifi and Fuzzlet it was. *Sigh*.

After running around for an hour, the puppies made their way back over to me, obviously tired and somehow already knowing I was their dad and that I wanted to take care of them.

So I stood to scoop them into my arms, and when Seb patted his lounge chair in invitation, I sat in front of him and leaned back against him, cradling two wiggle worms in my arms.

With the puppies snuggling against me and my back against my viramore's chest, the two of us watched our family milling about the yard, laughing, teasing, playing, and chatting together. Sometimes I honestly couldn't believe how much time had passed and just how large our family had grown.

My viramore and I were the luckiest people in the world to have such an amazing family.

"I love you, Ailin."

"I love you too, baby." I twisted around to give him a soft kiss. "So fucking much."

He sent me a soft smile and hugged me tighter around the waist.

Then Fuzzlet wiggled around, climbed my shoulder, and started licking the crap out of him.

I laughed, and Seb sighed, saying, "This is my life now. I've done this to myself." He shook his head at me. "You're a chaos gremlin."

That made me laugh again. "You love it."

"Uh-huh. Sure, I do."

I smiled to myself and hugged the puppies tight, still surprised and so damn happy that Seb had actually gone out and bought me these cuties. They started wiggling around, already bored of napping on me. So I set them on the ground, and Fifi jumped on top of Fuzzlet, and the pair went rolling around in the grass, leaving burnt spots every now and then.

Seb tightened his hold on me and rested his chin on my shoulder. "I'm not gonna say you can't bring them in our bed because I know you're going to, no matter what I say."

That was true, so I didn't deny it.

He huffed. "But I have one rule."

"What's that?"

"*You* are the one that has to take them out to potty in the middle of the night. I'm not doing it."

That made me grin. "I suppose I can do that."

He waited a beat. "I heard a *but* in that sentence."

I snorted. "*But* I know you're going to end up doing it with me anyway, so I don't even know why you're bothering."

He sighed. "You know, sometimes you're a real asshole."

"Yep."

He chuckled and buried his face in the crook of my neck. "You wanna know why I got you the puppies?"

"Because you love me."

"Yes, but other than that."

"Uh, I have no idea."

He paused. "Because I knew you were gonna try to convince me to adopt more kids after you played Santa, so I figured this would stop you."

I burst out laughing. "Having hellhound puppies is going to be nearly as bad. They're seriously big, giant babies and way more needy than a regular dog. They stay puppies for longer too."

"Yeah, I'm seeing that."

I hugged his arms across my belly. "Nice try, though."

"Thanks."

After a few minutes, I asked, "Soooo... do you think you might want more kids in the future?"

He groaned loudly. "Whhhhyyy do I do this to myself? Why the fuck did I bring it up?"

I laughed and patted his hand. "I'm only joking... mostly."

"Ailin?"

"Yeah?"

"You're not allowed to adopt anything or any*one* else while we have puppies in the house."

"What about when they're all grown up and officially out of the puppy stage?"

He sighed like he was very put out. "We'll... talk about it then, but it's not gonna be actual children. But maybe a... bunny or a cat or something like that."

That meant I had a few years to convince him. I could totally wear him down by then. "Fine."

"Hm. Didn't expect you to agree like that."

"What can I say? You got me puppies and put me in the best mood ever."

He laughed and kissed my temple. "Glad you're in a good mood because you better go grab that little guy before he hops up on the food table."

I looked at the food table with wide eyes. "Oh shit!"

Pulling out of Seb's arms, I ran for the little hellhound while my viramore laughed it up behind me. And when he started cracking up because I had to chase the little booger around the yard because he had a paper plate in his mouth, I couldn't help but laugh along with him.

A lot of the kids laughed too.

What a perfect way to celebrate the holiday with the love of my life and our very big, very awesome family all together and filled to the brim with love... and lots of laughing at my expense.

I couldn't have asked for a better holiday.

Thank you so much for reading *Seb & Ailin: Case of the Murderous Mistletoe*! I hope you enjoyed visiting with the Ellwoods as much as I did.

If you'd like more Seb & Ailin adventures, check out my Patreon.

And if you'd like to read the beginning of Seb and Ailin's story and read many of their kids' love stories, you can find the Ellwood/Brinnswick reading order HERE.

Thank You!

Thank you to each and every person who read *Murderous Mistletoe*. I truly appreciate it. I really hope you enjoyed going with Seb & A on a new adventure. The two of them hold a very special place in my heart and are always so much fun to write.

Thank you to my patrons! You guys have encouraged me and helped me in more ways than you know. I will be forever grateful for your kindness.

A special thanks to:

callie palmer, C Wilson, Sabrina Santore, Christine Wirth, Renae Fussell, Jenny Olsen, Danika , Ashley Bartz, Marielle Fernandez, Katelin MacVey, Whimsical Meerkat, Kelly Knight, Ashley Sellers, Lori Griff, Heidi , MarlesBells, Fei, chance wherley, Amelia, Nita Drumm, Katie, NeyNey, Stacey Cornwell, Eileen O'Brien Kernan, Kristin Fischer, Tammara Fort, Nicole, Brandi, Nichole Reeder, Yvonnee Gaynor, Jeannette Marsala, Rebecca, Michelle Thorne, Shaun Gannon, Susanne, Hillary Schommer, Tracy Cox, Lorene McLaughlin, MsDarkPhoenix, Amanda Parry, Lisa, Katherine Coleman, Becca Ison, Cristy Burchartz, Joy T, Melanie Rourke, kandice williams, and Shanna Reimer

About the Author

Michele is married to an awesome guy that puts up with her and all the burnt dinners she makes—hey, sometimes characters are a bit distracting, and who doesn't plot when they're supposed to be cooking? They live together in Baltimore, Maryland with two little monsters, a three-legged princess, a four-legged goofball, and a cutie with giant ears (aka their two kids, their two cats, and their dog). She hopes to rescue another cat soon, and if her hubby wouldn't kill her, she'd get more than one... and maybe a few more dogs as well.

She loves creating worlds filled with lots of love, chosen family, and of course, magic, but she also likes making the characters fight for that happy ending. She hopes to one day write all the stories in her head—even if there are too many to count!

MICHELE'S LINKS:

Website

Patreon

Facebook

Instagram

BookBub

Join Michele's Newsletter to keep up to date on my upcoming books!

Stop by for exclusives, updates, and lots of fun in Michele's Facebook Reader Group: Notaro's Haven.

Books by Michele Notaro

Brinnswick: Tales From Gauhala: (Urban Fantasy Romance)

The Witch's Grumpy Dragon

The Vampire's Delicious Fae

Fortune Favors the Fae: (Urban Fantasy Romance)

The Wolf's (Un)Lucky Fae (Remi Ellwood & Belryn Bixidor's story)

The Magi Accounts: (Urban Fantasy Romance)

The Scars That Bind Us

The Shackles That Hold Us

A Purpose That Restores Us

A Ruse To Unchain Us

Only Unity Will Spare Us

The Magi Accounts Companion Stories: (Urban Fantasy Romance)

Our Hearts That Tie Us
A Kiss To Revive Me
A Date To Impress Him
A Holiday To Sustain Us
An Embrace To Hearten Me
A Heart to Revitalize Me

The Ellwood Chronicles: (Witch Romance)
The Witch's Seal
The Enchanter's Flame
The Enchanter's Soul
The Witch's Blood
The Enchanter's Heart
The Enchanter's New Kids
The Ellwood Chronicles Bonus Scenes

The Brinnswick Chronicles: (Witch Romance)
Thayer
Nikolai
Basil
Jorah
Talon

A Brinnswick Story: (Supernatural Romance)
The Human's Incubus
There's A Bat In My Room!

RIPP: (Paranormal Romance collab with Sammi Cee)
The Ghost in the Emerald Cabin

Coldburgh Train Station

Reclaiming Hope: (Shifter Romance)
How We Survive
Rescuing His Heart
Free Novella: *First Moon Festival*
Keeping Them Unseen
Finding Our Home

Beyond the Realm: Remember: (Mage Romance)
Rueberry Orchard

Kingdoms of Pelas: (Fantasy Harem Collab with Michelle Frost)
Zyon
Tisak

Warlock Romances:
Wishing On A Dream
Building on a Hope

The Taoree Trilogy: (Alien MM Fiction)
Taoree
Independents
Dissolution

The Brotherhood of Ormarr: (Dragon Rider Romance)
Book 1: *Azaran* (by Jacki James)
Book 2: *Zale* (by Michelle Frost)
Book 3: *Eeli* (by Bobbie Rayne & Steph Marie)

Book 4: *Malachite* (by Michele Notaro & Sammi Cee)

Finding My Forever: (Contemporary Romance)
Everything In Between
A Little Bit Broken
Left Behind
A True Fit

A Finding My Forever Short Story: (Contemporary Romance)
Falling In Time
A Valentine's Tail

Flash Me Photos: (Contemporary Romance)
Love, Never-Ending

The Fate of Love Series: (Contemporary Romance)
Always You

My Forever: (Contemporary Romance)
Color My Kiss
Luck of the Ship

Interlocking Fragments: (Contemporary Romance Collab with Sammi Cee)
Heart Strain
Digging Deeper
Liberating Love
Seeking Freedom

Audiobooks:

The Enchanter's Flame

The Enchanter's Soul

The Witch's Blood

The Enchanter's Heart

How We Survive

Rescuing His Heart

Rueberry Orchard

Thayer

The Scars That Bind Us

A Kiss To Revive Me

The Shackles That Hold Us

A Date To Impress Him

A Purpose That Restores Us

A Ruse To Unchain Us

Only Unity Will Spare Us

A Wolf's (Un)Lucky Fae

A Holiday To Sustain Us

My Young Adult Books

Under the Name Bobbie Rayne

The Crazy Adventures of Cass & Star: **(Paranormal Young Adult)**

do you think we should've glued it first?

More to come in this series...

The Triumphs of the Everette Brothers: **(Contemporary YA collab with Steph Marie)**

Genuinely Extraordinary

More to come in this series...

The Brotherhood of Ormarr: **(Paranormal NA collab with Steph Marie)**

Book 3: _Eeli_

This is a complete series written with a group of authors.

Made in the USA
Columbia, SC
24 December 2024

48655987R10117